Anita Hendy's

Girl Called Molly

Anita Hendy ©

Published by
Anita Hendy
Prefix 0-9549641
Ballyteague Sth,
Kilmeague,
Naas,
Co. Kildare,
Ireland.

December 2006
1st Edition.

ISBN 0-9549641-3-6

Check out Anita's Web Site www.anitahendy.com

This book is the first part in a Trilogy
by Anita Hendy
The other two books are called
'The Furlong Spirit'
'Father William'

'This 'Trilogy' is dedicated to
any reader whose lovely character
may have been hurt, & to whom Christian comfort
is weakened by the destructive influence of evil.
This 'Trilogy' was written so
that the grace of holiness may become a visible light
in all our eyes, giving love, forgiveness and peace
to the gentle hearts of all peoples in this beautiful world.'

Anita Hendy 2006

CHAPTER ONE

A storm raged across the city of Dublin. Heavy dark clouds rolled over the majestic tower of Christ Church. Under the stone arch people huddled for shelter. Old and new buildings were at the mercy of the ferocious winds. The rain lashed down on the streets as if they were being punished for unknown deeds. By three a.m. the streets were deserted, the people beaten back behind the terraced doors and windows.

As the black clouds rolled out towards Dublin Bay the streets now calm were scattered with broken boughs and dead leaves. Newspapers, which only hours before held hot comforting chips, now lay wet and soggy in the gutters.

But with the splendid dawn a calmness descended on the city. The light from the ever-rising sun began tipping and bouncing off the large windows and lintels of the Georgian doors, which made up the wonderful houses of Henrietta Street.

On another street people making their way silently to work passed McDermott's Fish Shop on the corner. It was a quaint little shop that had been part of their street for three generations.

The heavy shutters were being removed as the horse and cart boys noisily rolled past and the owner, J. J. McDermott was busy putting barrels out on the pavement. Beside the shop, the door of a red brick terraced house opened slowly, as if to give a final check that it was safe to do so, and a little girl came tripping out the door. Her long strawberry blonde curls cascading over her shoulders in a burst of gold were set alight by the morning sun.

Her aunt Jessie McDermott, short in height, heavily built, with no grace of movement, followed the child down the steps and proceeded to tie the strings of a pink bonnet under her pert little chin. Molly wriggled determined to be free of the unwanted object and said,

'No Auntie, I want the wind to play in my hair'.

Aunt Jessie watched the child run down the pavement, and a slight tension rippled across her plain worried face. The strain of rearing such an unusual child was beginning to show and it had not been easy. She thought of that terrible sad night ten years earlier when

Jessie's sister-in-law had begged her to take care of her newborn baby girl.

Jessie had hesitated, what on earth did she know about babies? She would have to discuss it with her husband J. J.

But the dying girl had grabbed her hand and held it tightly. She looked soul-searchingly into her eyes and said:

'Promise me, you've got to promise me you're the only one I can count on.'

So Jessie promised, and her sister-in-law died happy in the knowledge that her baby would be safe. It was still a mystery why she had died and Jessie's brother Mick, the baby's father, never got over it.

Jessie's own marriage was childless and in a way Molly fulfilled a need in her. J. J. her husband, was a tall thin man with sharp features.

He had come up the hard way and escaped a life of severe poverty when he inherited the fish shop from his Uncle Sean. A self educated man, drawing from life's experiences rather than books, his daily life was one of strict routine and business. He took great pride in his shop, keeping it spic and span, a place for everything and everything in its place. His love of football and hurling brought him to the pub most nights, but more for conversation than the drink. After thirty years of marriage, he still could not get it all his own way on the domestic front. He accepted his lot in life but behind it lay a very sensitive man. Their marriage never reached heights of great passion.

J. J. seemed unaware of them and Jessie, well, she could only dream about them. Like everything else in life, he accepted Molly's existence and neither added to or took from it.

By now, the child had rounded the corner and was out of sight. A small clump of leaves rose up and danced at her feet. Meeting with her best friend Roseanne always made her smile, today was no exception. Racing up to Molly, her eyes protruding with excitement, Roseanne could not wait to tell how the storm had forced her to take refuge under her bed the night before. She talked ever so fast, while jumping up and down, and finding time to twiddle her little thumb in her short black hair. Together the two friends walked on as the traffic began pouring on to the road.

Lorries, buses and milk carts all seemed to compete to make the most noise. The little girls turned towards the shop windows to avoid the black smelly fumes belching out of the exhaust pipes. With their eyes transfixed on the beautiful dresses being displayed on the dummies standing life-like in the windows, they were suddenly jolted back to reality by the screeching of the brakes from the No. 6 and 8 buses. Turning into the next street, they saw familiar twin boys leaning against the black iron railings. They were so engrossed in conversation that they were oblivious to the noisy traffic. As the girls drew nearer, they could see that Seamus the funny one, was tying knots in the string of his conker. Jumping into their path he proudly proclaimed,

'Hey girls, guess how long it would take you to get these knots out of my string?'

Roseanne burst out giggling.

'I wouldn't touch your bleedin' string Seamus, get them out yerself.'

Molly was thinking maybe she could get them out by the time she reached school. But just then, Seamus pulled at the string and all the knots disappeared to the girls amazement. Then he turned and walked proudly away with the string dangling from his overstuffed pocket, and tipping his socks which lay in clumps on the top . of his boots. William, his brother, smiled shyly at the girls, and whistling a tune, picked up his bag and followed his brother down the road.

The little procession of four continued slowly towards the school. The echo of more children could be heard underneath the arch of the bridge. The skipping rope resounded with a crack on the pavement and the accompanying rhyme was chanted with military precision.

Tinker, Tailor, Soldier, Sailor
Rich man, Poor man,
Beggarman, Thief.

Concepta Moore, a rather rough girl, and the school bully, roared at the four friends as they passed.

'Hey youse, I've just done 100 skips. Bet ya can't beat that.' She pointed at Molly as she had always been jealous of the pretty girl.

Dropping her bag slowly, Molly moved reluctantly towards the rope. The others formed a semi-circle behind her in an effort to lend their support. Lifting her right leg she began to skip. When she had reached 35 skips she became quite breathless and her little face turned bright crimson Suddenly, the wind rose up and encircled her feet as if to form an invisible spring beneath her. Her breathing became effortless as the breeze cooled her face. To everyone's amazement she continued skipping. The children gathered around her chanting the numbers 98, 99, 100.

Concepta Moore became agitated and shouted 'That's enough, we have ta go now.'

Molly skipped another 10 skips and then passed everyone out as she raced to the school gates.

The children ran after her delighting in the fact that she had got the better of the school bully.

CHAPTER TWO

The big grey doors of No. 28 closed behind Seamus and William as they arrived home. Their mother Hattie Thornton did not see them come in as she was busy choosing a fabric for some new curtains she was about to order.

Having come from a big farm in Co. Wexford, Hattie found living in Dublin very exciting. Her parents had sent her to a boarding school in Eccles Street, which was run by the Dominican Sisters.

She had met her late husband James Thornton at a birthday party when she was 18. He was studying Business Studies at Trinity College and it was love at first sight. From then on he lavished all his attentions on her and after a long courtship and a short engagement they were married. Blessed with twin sons in the fifth year of marriage, their lives seemed complete. A petite woman, with olive skin and brown eyes, Hattie's beauty spot being meticulously painted on her right cheek, could move a fraction or two from day to day. Since her husband's death two years ago, she now felt a great need to indulge in her frivolous ways. As well as being an accountant in Guinness Brewery, James had also been a shareholder in the company. His death had left Hattie extremely wealthy and after years of strict budgeting Hattie could now fly high with her diary always being full of engagements

The two boys were no problem as Julie, their nanny and housekeeper, was always on hand to sort them out. Besides Hattie had just entered the stage of her life where nature plays its final trick on womanhood, the menopause. The mischievous escapades of the boys always coincided with the hot flushes and Hattie would frequently retire with blinding headaches to her bedroom leaving strict instructions that she was not to be disturbed.

Not being identical twins, the two boys also had vast differences in their characters. Seamus took on the role of 'man of the house' when his father died. He had to put up with his mother's hypochondriac ways and her constant longing for cigarettes. If only he had a penny for all the times she sent him to the shop for 'Craven As'.

The first two fingers of her right hand were a darker shade than the rest. Her red painted lips could encircle the cork tipped cigarette with a forceful caress. Then drawing the smoke deep into her lungs, she would give a sigh of relief, then exhale the smoke high into the air. Being advanced for his tender years, Seamus knew these cigarettes were a crutch for something that was missing in his mother's life. He naturally presumed it was his Father.

William, known as Willie, looked up to Seamus and seemed to walk in his shadow. He was a very observant child. His brown eyes seemed to have an almost spiritual depth and understanding, which came more from his senses than from his intelligence.

Never was this more obvious than on one hot afternoon in June when William, Seamus, Roseanne and Molly went exploring. An abandoned army camp was the target for many of the local children. The big iron gate had a heavy lock and chain just for the purpose of keeping out unwanted visitors. But the children had made their own entrance further down through a small hole in the hedge. Once inside, the buildings in a semi-circle towered over them . Wild bushes and thorny weeds protruded almost finger-like from windows and doors as if trying to grab them. But they ventured on through the long grass with the boys taking the lead and the girls bringing up the rear.

Now and again their bare legs would get pricked by thistles or stung by nettles, but soon, however, they reached the clearing in front of the red brick houses.

Seamus was first into the abandoned house. He stood still in the semi-darkness of the building, his eyes squinting to adjust from the bright sunshine outside. Suddenly he saw a shadow move and could just make out the figure of a man.

Thinking it was a workman he called to the others. Then the smell of alcohol drifted towards him. A dirty big tramp jumped up quickly to his feet, and with his long coat flying roared at the children 'Get out, get out of this place or I'll bleedin' kill yeeze.'

Seamus did not have to be told twice. His young shocked face drained of all colour and he turned to the others and shouted 'Run, run.'

The children ran as if the devil himself was chasing them. Seamus was afraid to turn around in case the monster might grab him from behind. The children ran and were just in sight of the hedge when suddenly Molly tripped and fell. Her hand came down on some broken glass hidden among other bits of rubbish. Large drops of blood flowed bright red on the green grass. Roseanne, on seeing this, screamed at the top of her voice and froze on the spot. Seamus and William turned back to rescue their friend. Tears streamed down Molly's face. Seamus took his handkerchief from

his pocket and tied it tightly around her hand to stop the bleeding while William went over to Roseanne. She was shaking and still screaming.

He held her tightly, gently stroking her hair and repeating over and over again that Molly would be all right. He knew he could depend on his brother to fix it.

A little later they were a sorry, pitiful sight as they helped each other through the hedge. They were so glad to be back on the road again, that they pledged never to return.

On the way home Molly turned to Seamus and said wistfully: 'Will you be a doctor when you grow up Seamus?'

'Why would you like me to be a doctor, Molly?' he asked curiously.

'So when I get sick you can save me.'

Putting his arm around her protectively he smiled as he replied 'Of course I will.'

Overhearing this, William felt a strange shiver run up his spine. Molly's question scared him just as much as Seamus's reply. He was the first to notice how the wind seemed to follow her and he knew there was something special about her.

Of course his mother had always said that the other children were of an inferior class. What was it she called them, oh yes, 'scruff. How often had he heard her say

'You shouldn't play with those children.' But being forbidden to play with them only made him want to so very much. He often wondered why all the nice children had to be 'scruff' and the others just plain boring. Right now none of it seemed to matter, as he was with Molly and Roseanne, and this was the only place in the whole world he wanted to be.

CHAPTER THREE

After that little episode Molly's activities were curtailed. During the school holidays she would accompany her Uncle J. J. on the fish round while Jessie kept very busy in the shop. Molly found it hard to talk to Uncle J .J. He was usually in a world of his own that existed long before she was born. But she listened as he went on and on about what life was like during the war. The shortage of food and how it was rationed.

'You don't know how lucky you are my girl, why in my day a two pound pot of jam would have to last a whole week and that between eight of us.'

He prided himself on his work and was heard to remark on more than one occasion:

'Jeepers, if every man in Ireland was as good as me this would be a great little country.'

Every Monday and Thursday they would load up the little Thames van with fresh plaice, haddock, mackerel etc. and head out on the coast road. J.J's regular customers were always pleased to see him coming and he had to have a chat with each one. Molly suffered the bumps and stops and starts because she knew that by 1 p.m. the van would eventually stop and they could enjoy the tasty tea and sandwiches Jessie had packed fresh for them that morning.

J.J.'s favourite spot for lunch was on the summit of Howth Head. Parking his van in the usual spot, Molly would jump out and stand on the edge of the cliff. The wind would caress her legs and body and lift her hair. Looking out across the Irish Sea, her thoughts would turn towards her father.

Mick McCoy was born in Ringsend, the eldest son of a docker, he was working in Bolands Mill when he married Molly's mother. They lived in a little red brick corporation house until she was born, but after her mother died, he disappeared. Three years later, Jessie, his sister, received a letter saying he had gone to sea. What Jessie did not tell Molly was that he blamed the baby for his wife's death. On that fateful night Jessie had walked down the stairs with the new-born in her arms. She had asked Mick what name should she christen it.

With tears of anger rolling down his face he replied, 'My Molly's gone, that baby took her life, now let her take her name,' and with that he left the house and was never seen again.

Molly knew her father was a seafaring man, but she could not understand the fact that he never wrote any letters or sent her presents for her birthday or at Christmas.

She knew what her parents had looked like as she would often spend precious time staring at the only photographs she had of them. She would make up stories as to how they met and fell in love.

Tracing her fingers over their dear faces, she would try and touch the untouchable. Then, with a heavy heart she would eventually fall asleep, the photographs clutched tightly to her tiny chest. Jessie would remove them gently when she tiptoed in to say goodnight.

But today, looking out across the ocean, she was thinking that it all seemed so hopeless that she would ever see her father or hear his voice, and for once, when JJ. called her back to the van, she was relieved to be going home.

CHAPTER FOUR

The children loved being together and their school work was excellent, but they hated the headmaster, Mr. Walkerton. His tall thin skeletal frame had just enough flesh to cover it without an inch to spare. His dark-rimmed glasses made his black eyebrows and eyes appear menacing. His tweed jacket with leather patched elbows looked like he had slept in it, and his matching hat hung limply on his head. His daunting appearance and dominating air was not to be challenged, especially by children.

Every morning on arriving in the classroom he would hang his hat on a short nail at the back of the door. The last child into the room would have to shut the door gently or Walkerton would be standing with his cane to the ready. Should the door bang and the hat fall, he would raise his arm and the cane would come down on the child responsible. Trembling and shaking the little youngster would struggle to try and hang it back on the nail. But whenever Walkerton himself came through the door and knocked the hat, Timothy Phelan was appointed to pick it up for him.

His anger was usually taken out on the Molloy sisters. He constantly picked on them as they were poor and slow at learning. How the children would cringe as he regularly called them up to the front of the class. Then he would lay them one at a time across his boney knees. Lifting up their dresses, he would expose the soft white flesh of their thighs. The girls would squeeze their eyes tightly as they heard the swish of the cane fly through the air and crack painfully down on their legs. Within seconds, the blue and red marks would appear. When Walkerton was satisfied, he would order them to rejoin their class-mates.

On many such occasions the Molloy girls were heard to say 'He will not make me cry.'

One calm summer day during sums class Molly's nose began to trickle. This cold had been coming on for a few days now, but today, it seemed there was a tap in her head that someone had forgotten to turn off. Walkerton was writing on the blackboard with his back to the class and called for complete silence. But her nose refused to stop trickling. She tried sniffing and used both her sleeves, but the wool was rough and pretty soon her tender young skin began to sting. She knew the handkerchief Aunt Hattie insisted she bring to school was in the desk but was reluctant to take it out. The lid of the desk squeaked and she dare not make a noise. She had been warned.

Then she thought ' If I open it very slowly maybe it won't creak so much.'

Inch by inch she lifted the lid until she could see the hankie. Slipping her hand in she caught it and was taking it out slowly when Walkerton gave a loud cough. The noise caused her hand to slip and the lid came down with an unmerciful bang. Walkerton jumped and nervously broke his chalk.

'Who made that noise?' he shouted.

The children kept their heads down and remained silent.

'Whoever it was better own up or you're all in trouble.'

Molly's stomach tightened and she thought she would be sick. Her heart was beating so loudly that she thought everyone in the room could hear it. Slowly she raised her hand in the air

'Come up here now Miss Malone' he said tapping his foot impatiently on the floor. Just as slowly as she had raised her hand she stood up from her seat. Her eyes filled with fearful tears and she could hardly see. Walking towards her scowling teacher she touched each desk with her fingertips, every step was an eternity. As she drew closer to him he suddenly reached out and grabbed her roughly pulling her down onto his knees. Then holding her fast with one hand he pulled back her dress and raised the cane.

Suddenly the door burst open and a powerful gust of wind ripped through the classroom. The maps lifted off the walls and the school books were flung to the floor. The windows rattled noisily and the children screamed. With his glasses blown from his eyes, Walkerton dropped the cane and released his hold on Molly. He tried to stand up but was immediately flung backwards against the blackboard. With his bryl-creamed hair standing on edge, he landed in an undignified heap on the floor. When Molly realized she was free, she walked calmly back to her desk. Then as quickly as it came, the wind dispersed and everything calmed down. The other children stood open-mouthed in amazement. They knew now for sure that there was something very special about her. Walkerton picked himself up off the floor.

Unable to carry on with the sums class he told the children in a faltering voice to take out their reading books. Still shaking he crossed the room and closed the door. Picking up his hat for the first time ever he hung it back on the nail. Then trying to coax his wisps of hair back into position he scratched his head and muttered to himself, 'What the hell was that?'

CHAPTER FIVE

School days fly and so it was for Molly and her friends. Her final year had come round. By now the four young people had become inseparable. The last day of school was a joyous one.

The sun streamed in through the large windows. The birds sang sweetly in the old oak trees standing majestically in the school grounds. As the bell rang the boys and girls burst through the doors and bounded down the steps. Like prisoners discarding their fetters they threw their books high in the air. They had a whole summer ahead of them. But then again they had a whole life-time ahead of them. This realization was reflected by the brilliant joyful smiles on all their young faces.

Roseanne had secured a job in Bewley's coffee shop on Grafton Street. This famous restaurant was renowned throughout Ireland. Waitressing was what Roseanne was suited to most as her bubbly personality and cheery disposition would cheer up any customer. However, William and Seamus more ambitiously were heading off to Belvedere College. Run by the Jesuits, its past pupils were very famous people indeed. Hattie was proud that her two fine sons would be following in their father's footsteps. If only he was alive today to see them, he would have been a proud man.

However, Molly was needed at home in the fish shop. It was here on the fourth day of September that Seamus and William found her when they came to say goodbye. They had a wonderful summer doing the usual things like swimming, picnics and racing, the highlight that year was the Thornton twins thirteenth birthday party. But now, with the leaves turning a golden brown and the evenings drawing in, summer was fast becoming another lovely memory to be stored up and relived in later years. Dressed in their identical uniforms and heading off to a new school, they had a chance to make new friends. It was very exciting yet very scary. Molly was impressed when she saw them. They looked so smart. Seamus awkwardly pulled an object from his pocket. It was a necklace made from knotted strips of leather.

'This is for you Molly, I made it myself, don't forget to write to me, okay.'

'Why its beautiful, thank you. I'll keep it always and of course I'll write.'

She reached up and kissed his cheek. He bent his head and looked bashfully down at the floor.

William touched her arm, and as she turned he pulled a flower from behind his back. It was a rose, perfectly formed, with the stem wrapped in brown paper. 'I picked this for you, its not much I know .. .'

Molly buried her face in it, and delighting in its scent she inhaled deeply.

'Thanks William' she said smiling.

'I know you love roses and don't forget to write to me too.'

'Of course I won't,' she said, planting another kiss on his cheek.

The tenderness of the moment was broken when a rather high pitched voice was heard calling them from the street. Hattie, as usual, was anxious to get going.

'Better go now,' said Seamus, 'mustn't keep mother waiting.'

They turned and walked awkwardly to the car.

Molly walked with them to the door as she fought to hold back the tears. Leaning on the door post, she held the rose close to her face while she clutched the necklace in her other hand. Never, in all her life, did she feel so loved and so very lonely all at the same time.

Some days were long for Molly and some days shorter in the little fish shop. As if the ocean itself was underfoot, the old blue tiles on the floor brought a cold atmosphere to the shop.

There was no shortage of fish, with the fishing vessels pulling in and out of Howth Harbour regularly. The odour of fish lay heavy in the air. Molly's apron was constantly smeared with fish blood and entrails, but she had become accustomed to it. She would play games in the quiet times when she was not busy. She would imagine that she was a mermaid princess and the shop was her sea palace, with the fishes her subjects. As they lay in their boxes with their large eyeballs protruding and their mouths open, she would point to them with a stick and say; 'Sir Mackerel, you must not stare like that as your Princess walks by, show a little respect', or she would line them up in perfect order like fish soldiers on parade. Her make-believe world would end, however, when the bells jangled on the shop door and the customers came in.

Dealing with customers was a daily learning experience. Many but not all rich folk would breeze in the door as if they owned the place. Looking down their noses, they would point with their gloved finger what they wished to buy as if not to be contaminated. They spoke to Molly as to a servant and demanded to know if the fish was fresh.

As she wrapped their purchases they watched her carefully. This made her nervous. Never carrying any money she would always hear the familiar line, 'Put it down in the book my girl ' and then just as haughtily as they entered they would depart.

In contrast, middleclass people would usual enter with a smile and greeting. Cracking jokes and teasing Molly they would pick up the fish, examine it carefully, then knowing the best value for money they would make their purchases. Having large families, budgeting was high on their list of priorities. Always paying in cash they would leave the shop feeling quite satisfied.

Then there was always the poor.

Unlike the other two groups they had little or no money. Pressing their hungry faces against the window their sad expressions would peer through the little panes of glass. Then, timidly they would creep into the shop, almost afraid to enter, with hunger drivingthem on. Their dirty bare feet looked vulnerable on the cold hard floor, and in a quiet whisper they would hopefully ask: 'Missus, could we have any of your fish that's leftover?'

Deep in her heart Molly would feel for these people.

She wanted to protect them from the world, but they were so many and she felt totally inadequate.

Quickly gathering fish heads, tails, and bones, to make fish soup with, she would also throw a decent piece of mackerel into the parcel. Wrapping them up in paper she would place them into their thin outstretched arms. They would bless her and thank her, and thank and bless her as they ran quickly from the shop. Watching them Molly always felt that she was the poorer one as they had great courage in the face of hunger.

But it was the gossips that Molly found most difficult to tolerate. Women who seemed to have nothing between their ears and less to do, would huddle in the comer like a group of hens. She would hear them say'Did you hear about your wan?', and 'Wait 'till I tell ya.'

Then, exhausting the list of people they knew they would eventually turn their attention on Molly.

She could feel their eyes piercing into the back of her head. Turning, she would notice a false smile on their lips and she would hear them say, 'Well dearie, don't you look well today.'

The sarcasm in their voices made her feel very uncomfortable and she was glad when they eventually left with their purchases.

CHAPTER SIX

On Saturday evening at 6 p.m. the shutters would come down and Molly's weekend would begin. The tired threesome would sit down to a hearty fry-up of sausages, rashers, black and white pudding and eggs. Jessie would produce some mouth-watering brown soda bread and it would be all washed down with a pot of Barry's tea. J.J. had extended his fish round to five days a week and he delighted in telling the two women yarns and jokes about his new customers.

Putting his tired swollen feet up on the old wooden footstool and folding his hands behind his head he would enquire: '1 hope your wrapping those bits of fish-ends in newspapers and not in me good wrapping paper Molly? Newspaper is good enough for the likes of them beggars. We don't want decent people to think we are giving good fish away for nothing. I have rents and taxes to pay and God knows they're crippling me.'

'Oh yes Uncle,' replied Molly.

'Ah yer a good wee girl, isn't she Jess?'

Jessie smiled to herself, it went without saying how much she thought of her.

After supper J.J. was first into the big cast iron bath which stood on four feet fashioned like lions paws. While he soaked he sang the same song 'Yes, Jesus loves me; Yes, Jesus loves me;

Yes, Jesus loves me for the bible tells me so.'

When the words ended he would continue to whistle the same tune. Emerging from the bathroom a half an hour later, his face shone like a new penny.

'Your turn now Molly and don't take all night in there. Jessie has to have her turn too,' and he would slap the towel against her bum as she walked past.

With her towels, soap, powder and perfume all gathered up in her arms Molly would move quickly towards the bathroom. The latch on the door clicked shut and she was now in a room nobody else could enter. Placing her toiletries on the window sill, she started removing her clothes. Oh, the freedom to stand completely naked and feel safe to do so.

As the steam rose up from the brass taps she wiped it away from the long mirror. Catching a glimpse of her reflection she noticed how her body was changing lately. Her breasts were getting bigger as they stood out from her body. Her waist was getting slimmer and her hips more round. Dark hair was appearing below her navel and she could swear blind she'd grown an inch or two in the last couple of weeks. These changes filled her with wonder and excitement. She liked her body. She liked the fact she was becoming a woman. The warm water crept up slowly as she descended into it. A shiver of relaxation enveloped her and she lay down completely immersed in it. When she emerged twenty minutes later from the bathroom her body was softand tingling.

Aunt Jessie was last to bathe, and while she did Molly perched herself in front of the coal fire at J.J.'s feet. There she finger-dried her long hair leaning against J.J. knees as he reclined in the armchair. His old pipe sticking out from the corner of his mouth sent puffs of smoke into the room. Molly liked the smell of the tobacco and did not complain. Not frequenting the pub on Saturday nights, J.J. preferred to stay in and listen to Ceili music on the little wooden wireless. Molly enjoyed the music but it did not excite her spirit. She always sensed somewhere she would find what would do this, but when and where it would happen she did not know.

Usually she was the first one to go to bed but tonight it was J.J. who unexpectedly retired early.

This gave Molly the opportunity she had been waiting for. There was so much she wanted to ask Aunt Jessie but the right moment never came round until now.

Not being capable of dodging direct questions Jessie responded positively when she asked her:

'Why did my mother die?'

Looking straight into her eyes Jessie knew she could not lie.

'Your mother died when she was young. Just after you were born.'

And what about Granny? When did she die?'

'Another difficult one,' thought Jessie.

'Why all the questions Molly?'

'Well, I overheard a conversation in the shop, the women were whispering about me.'

'What did they say?'

They said babies were bad luck to the Malone's. What did they mean Aunt Jessie?'

Blast those women any way,' thought Jessie. 'Couldn't they keep their big mouths shut

'Look,' she said aloud placing her hand on

Molly's shoulder, 'Your Granny died in childbirth as did so many others at that time. But that was years ago when there was not much medical knowledge about these things. Its different nowadays.'

Then looking up at the clock she exclaimed;

'Goodness gracious is that the time? Best go to bed now, we have to be up bright and early for Mass in the morning. We'll talk about this again some other night eh?

'But Auntie ...' persisted Molly.

'Now I said that's enough, bed'.

Molly thought it best leave well enough alone.

There was no point in asking Aunt Jessie why she herself had no children. Getting up from the floor she began to gather up her toiletries. Then leaning over, she kissed Jessie on the cheek and went reluctantly up to bed.

CHAPTER SEVEN

Two years later Dublin City was held fast in the hard grip of winter. In the air the smell of burning coal hung suspended as if by invisible threads. The street lamps were lit by 5 p.m. Molly was wearing extra clothes to work but despite this her feet and hands were constantly pinched by the cold. She got no sympathy from J.J. when she complained, 'Cold! shur' that's not cold. Why in my day winters were so cold that you'd have to put your feet into warm dung to prevent frostbite. I remember going to school with a sod of turf under me arm and so did the other children just to keep the fire in the school going. Aye, they were bad winters alright.'

Not really listening to her Uncle, Molly's thoughts turned instead towards Christmas. It would soon be here and William and Seamus would return again. She could not wait to tell be with them all her news.

When they walked into the fish shop the day before Christmas Eve, the twins were just as excited to see her. Molly rushed over to them with her arms open wide. But they jumped back quickly from her embrace saying;

'Watch it Molly, you'll get smelly fish guts on our school uniforms.'

Stopped in her tracks her smile disappeared as she stepped back. Feelings of shame and embarrassment rose up inside her as she looked down at her soiled apron. Unaware of this the young teenagers chatted on about their new school, their new friends and their new teachers. Watching them closely she noticed how Seamus's voice was deeper and there were tiny dark hairs on his chin, rather like fluff. William had grown a little taller too and a gold pin inserted under their collars gave them both a hint of haughtiness. But they both looked very well.

'Well Molly,' said William 'You must have a lot to tell us eh?'

Just hours ago this was the case but not now.

Compared to their life, hers seemed rather boring.

'Roseanne is stepping out with Tom O'Brien, you remember him from school. Sometimes they call here to the shop.'

'Yeah, we remember him all right, a bit of a lug, but don't tell Roseanne we said so.'

The boys wandered around the shop and an awkward silence fell on the conversation. Then they suddenly remembered they had to visit other friends and promised to call back later. As they left the shop, William remarked to Seamus how pretty Molly was.

'1 think she's even prettier than ever,' replied Seamus. It was on his mind to return and talk to her alone. When he returned in the afternoon the shop was packed and she could just see him out of the corner of her eye. He winked at her from behind fat Mrs. O'Rourke's back and she blushed. When she looked up he was gone. As she was closing up shop, William also happened to stroll by offering to help carry the barrels and close shutters. He felt an excitement run through him whenever he brushed past her. This feeling made it awkward for him to talk, and in fact he ended up hardly saying a word. Molly was in a slight state of confusion when he left suddenly and hurried away. Her thoughts went over the events of the day. Here were the two boys she had known all her life, played games with, went exploring with, and now felt so embarrassed and confused in their company. Her awakening to their masculinity was a new experience and it made her suddenly become aware of her own femininity. She blushed as she recalled how their eyes would wander to her breasts and look quickly away. As she caught sight of her reflection in the cracked mirror at the back of the shop, she gave herself a good talking to.

'Now, listen here' she said to herself, 'You better calm down and pretend nothing is happening.' But really she did not feel convinced at all.

So on Sunday morning at 11 o'clock Mass the friends repeatedly kept stealing looks at each other across the pews. Aware of what was happening Hattie Thornton hurried the boys out of the church after Mass. She had nothing personal against the girl but her boys had more serious things to think about than a fishmonger's adopted daughter.

Christmas was Molly's favourite time of year. Even though it was a while since she believed in Santa Claus, it still held a magic for her. The lights twinkling in the streets and shops. The Christmas trees shimmering in the windows and people rushing about with parcels under their arms. But the carols were her favourite. When she heard the wonderful melodious harmonies of the voices of the choirs her soul lifted towards a heavenly vision of peace and goodwill towards everyone.

Aunt Jessie and Uncle J.J. hugged each other on Christmas morning as they excitedly watched Molly's eyes light up when she saw the a ladies Raleigh bike complete with basket, standing beside the Christmas tree.

'Oh, is this really for me?' she said, touching it carefully in case it might disappear. 'Oh thank you. I love it.' and the little family were quickly wrapped in a tight embrace.

'Can I go and show it to William, Seamus and Roseanne, Auntie?

'After dinner you can,' said Jessie 'Right now I need your help in the kitchen, I have a lot to do.' Later her friends were very impressed with her new bike and they all took turns trying it out. Things relaxed after Christmas day and everyone had fun. But the holidays went very quickly. The boys returned to school and Molly found herself once more behind the counter.

January was a quiet month and a complete anti-climax. It seemed to go on forever. Molly could not help thinking about the boys and their funny new ways. They had taken to standing up on the bus to let her sit down. When they sat down, she noticed how they pulled up the knees of their trousers just like J.J. did. They opened doors for her and they always covered their mouths when they coughed. Walking down the street with them, she was very aware that she was in the company of two young gentlemen.

CHAPTER EIGHT

By now the boys were writing letters to Molly on a regular basis and she in turn loved reading them. Her imagination would take her right into their school and everything they described. She would enter into it just as if she herself were there. She would always save the letters until she was alone in her room. Sitting cross-legged on the bed, she would read about their love of music and theatre and all the mischievous escapades they got up to. However between the lines she felt a seriousness creeping in to their lives. This stirred deep feelings in her but for what she did not know. When they wrote and said they would not be home for Easter she was very disappointed. Hattie was bringing them on a trip to London to see the sights. They would take in an opera at Covent Garden, and they were all going to stay with their cousins near Leicester Square.

Disappointment was written all over her face. She began to mope around the house, picking at her food, annoying at Aunt Jessie. One day Jessie decided she had enough. Something would have to be done. She waited until that night as J.J. was preparing for bed. In a gentle voice she began:

'J.J. I've been thinkin'.'

'Oh yes,' he replied as he undressed.

'Well,' continued Jessie, 'it seems to me we've been working Molly a little too hard. She's lookin' rather pale and her appetite is not as good as it was. She really could do with a half day off from the shop, what do you think? Now Wednesdays aren't that busy.'

'Good God woman, do you think I'm made of money,' he drawled as he nearly swallowed his false teeth in the effort of removing them.

'Well,' continued Jessie, 'if she gets sick you're goin' to have to pay someone to run the shop and full rate at that. Then see how much it will cost you.'

J. J. began to think, maybe Jessie had a point. But then women had an uncanny way of being right. Better save a penny than lose a pound and Wednesday afternoons were not that busy. Anyway his business was picking up nicely but it was best to keep that to himself.

'Okay, I suppose so, but she better make good use of her time off. I don't want her hanging around comers with those riff-raff layabouts that I have to hunt from my shop daily. You see she does something productive with her time.'

'Oh, I will J.J. don't worry about that, I'll tell her first thing in the morning.' and reaching up she switched off the bedside lamp.

When Roseanne heard about Molly's half day she grew very excited indeed. She could now bring her dearest friend to town. They would have such fun together. The two girls embraced each other with joy.

Boarding the 22 bus they sat down at the back in order to get a better view. Molly gave Roseanne a sharp dig in the ribs, certain that the bus conductor overheard her say: 'Don't ya love men in uniforms?'

Roseanne burst into a fit of giggles. Then an aroma of coffee filled the bus. Molly, remarking on this, made Roseanne laugh again and say: 'That's not coffee ye eejit, that's the hops from Guinness Brewery.'

'Whatever it was it smelt divine,' thought Molly.

The last stop was their stop and as they alighted a shout went up from a newspaper boy:' Herald or Mail.' Passing by the two girls almost jumped out of their skins. Observing this the boy gave them a cheeky grin and a flirty wink. But the girls were not impressed and with their noses up in the air they walked on. The breeze which followed Molly ruffled the papers on the stand and scattered them to the pavement. Scratching his head with his mouth open the boy looked after them in amazement.

Roseanne was in a half gallop pulling Molly by the hand up the street as she made a beeline for Brown Thomas department store. Her Tom O', had found employment there. As they walked through the large glass doors, they spotted him stacking shelves at the back of the shop. Catching sight of the two girls, he marched over with an air of importance. Giving them a mock bow he said courteously:

'May I be of service to you ladies?'

'Get up ya ejit.' said Roseanne looking around embarrassingly, 'You're makin' a show of us. You know Molly, don't ya?' 'Hello Molly,' said Tom O' and was about to say more when Roseanne pulled him to one side.

24

Molly was now standing alone in the centre of the shop. Her attention was drawn to her surroundings. The luxurious shop seemed to bring a sense of wonder to her. The rich soft deep wool car- pet was like a sponge under her feet. Jewellery and glass twinkled everywhere and Aladdin's Cave immediately sprung to mind. On each side of the store were two elegant staircases. Molly went over to them and, when she ascended or descended, she could not help but feel like Cinderella at the ball. 'Imagine' she thought 'actually getting paid to work here.'

Suddenly the fish shop seemed cold and grubby. Tom O' looked very smart in his suit and not at all like the scruffy boy she remembered in school. A shiny belt and buckle replaced his childish braces and he reminded her of the actor Alan Ladd. Roseanne rejoined her at the shoe counter.

Peering over her shoulder she said annoyingly;

'You'll never afford anything here Molly, lets go to Woolworths instead. We'll meet up with Tom O' later.'

Still stunned by the atmosphere in the store Molly stepped out on to Grafton Street. J.J. Aunt Jessie and the fish shop all disappeared. She suddenly had a whole new feeling about life. She watched the people walk up and down the street and said to herself: 'Yes, I want to be part of all this.'

Their next stop was Woolworths. Their eyes almost popped out of their heads when they saw all the goods on display. Checking the prices they knew they could afford to buy here. Molly saw a lovely brooch for 7/6. for her Aunt. But she remembered Jessie saying lately she really needed a new hair net. Maybe it would be better to get her something that she wanted. She would get the brooch next time. Anyway, the hair net was only 1/5d. For 2/6d Roseanne picked up a nice pen for Tom O's top pocket. She had noticed the other assistants carried pens and her Tom O' would be no exception. Then with their purchases under their arms Roseanne suggested a coffee break in Bewleys.

'Us waitresses can get coffee and cakes at half price you know.'

This was a favourite meeting place for rich and poor, student and teacher, young and old alike. Roseanne seemed to be quite popular with the other girls. Smiling, she returned to the table laden down with two cups of steaming coffee and four iced buns. This was

Molly's first taste of coffee. The warm black liquid hit the back of her throat, travelled down to her stomach, and a warm glow of satisfaction went right through her. She sipped it slowly to make it last. Inhaling the aroma, she wrapped her small hands tightly around the cup as if to prevent anyone taking the precious liquid from her. If this was heaven then she was in it. Looking around the restaurant she thought how easy it would be to imagine the stories behind the faces of all the people passing through. Later, feeling thoroughly refreshed, the young girls left Bewleys, strolled down the elegant Grafton Street, into the wider O'Connell Street, and down a busy Henry Street. Turning into Moore Street they found stalls and prams on both sides laden down with fresh fruit, vegetables, fish, and goods. The busy street echoed to the sound of Dublin women's unique strong voices competing against each other for trade.

'Get your fresh fish here 'Plug tobacco 2/s,'

'Watch your step there luv. ' said one woman pointing to a crate Molly was about to trip over. As Molly listened to the women she felt she here she was at the real heart and pulse of Dublin city. These women were the conquerors of the streets. With their convoy of prams, they headed from Smithfield Market at 5 a.m. every morning. Mothers, wives, sisters, daughters battling the elements and the traffic with a camaraderie and cheerfulness that could only be envied. But while Molly admired them, she did not really want to become like them. This was not for her, she wanted something more.

As the shops closed their shutters at 6 p.m. The girls made their way back up towards O'Connell Bridge and on to Grafton Street. Tom O' was waiting patiently for them outside the shop, ready to escort them to the Carlton Cinema. Norman Wisdom was showing and, as the girls took their seats inside Molly could not help feeling that she was playing gooseberry. However, she soon became so engrossed with the antics of the comedian that she forgot all about her two friends. After the show, while walking towards number 22 bus, she remarked how her tummy actually hurt from all the laughing.

'Oh Roseanne, I've had such a good time. thanks so much.' she said giving her friend a tight hug.'

'Oh we'll do it again next month,' said Roseanne and as Molly stepped on to the bus which would take her home, Roseanne and Tom

O' waved at their friend until she was out of sight. Arriving back at home Molly opened the front door gently and stepped into the hallway. Aunt Jessie was waiting up for her and waving her finger signalled her to proceed quietly up the stairs. She would catch up with all the news in the morning.

Not wanting to wake J.J. up Molly took off her shoes and skipped over the third step because it creaked. Once in her room she lay down on her bed. Gazing up at the ceiling she relived her day all over again. Then getting up she walked over to the window. Opening it she leaned out and looked at the many twinkling lights of a large city. She knew she was being drawn to the excitement of it all and that soon she would just have to experience it all over again.

CHAPTER NINE

William woke early. The warm summer air hung heavy in his room. Outside he could hear birds Singing high in the trees. He gave a long contented stretch and lay back on the pillows. Gazing up at the ceiling, his first thoughts were of Molly. In his mind's eye he could see her fabulous smile. and her lovely blue eyes. His heart swelled in his chest with happiness and he knew he would have to see her today. He needed to tell her how he felt and dared to hope that she might feel the same. After breakfast he pottered around his bedroom trying hard to concentrate on tidying it up, but every so often he found himself gazing out of the window thinking only of Molly. Later when he opened the door of the fish shop he caught sight of her 'basting' the fish with ice to keep them fresh. The day was hot, but she looked amazingly cool in her sleeveless frock. A gently breeze lifted her hair from her neck and she was humming a little tune. She looked up when he came in and smiled.

His heart lifted.

'Hello Molly, gosh it's warm.' he said timidly.

'Yes William, I'm fed up carrying in ice to keep the fish fresh. Where's Seamus?'

'Oh, he's still in bed I should imagine, the lazy thing. Anyway I'm glad he is because there's something I want to ask you. Would you like to come for a walk with me tonight? We could get some ice cream and maybe go to the pictures if there is something good on?'

Surprised at his question and not being able to think quickly enough she found herself saying 'Yes' before she realised she had said it. 'Right, that's great. I'll meet you at your house around seven, okay.?'

'Fine' said Molly smiling.

'Okay ... so ... em ... I'll see you then.'

He went to walk out the door casually but in his excitement he almost tripped. However once outside on the street there was no stopping his feet. He managed to bump into almost everyone on the pavement as he hurried home. his thoughts were racing.

'I'll be with Molly tonight, in a few hours.'

What would he do for those few hours. Still, it didn't matter nothing mattered only Molly.

As there were hardly any customers around due to the lovely sunshine Molly decided to close the shop early. She needed extra time to get ready for the evening ahead. A shiver of excitement ran through her too as she told Aunt Jessie about her date. Offering to run a bath for her. Jessie took a bottle of 4711 cologne from her drawer. It was funny how every Christmas J.J. would give her the same gift wrapped up in a white lace handkerchief. Still it did not matter, tonight was just a night to use it. Molly took extra care bathing and dressing and Jessie smiled as she heard singing from the bathroom. Downstairs in the kitchen she thought 'wouldn't it be marvellous if William and Molly fell in love.'

Her mind then losing the run of itself, began to think about the wedding, the house and even the children they might have. Molly would have a lifestyle that Jessie could only dream about. After all the Thornton's were not short of a bob or two. Suddenly the voices of two men broke into her thoughts and when she looked up she saw J.J. showing William into the sitting room. Jessie noticed how fresh faced he looked. Untying her apron she went to greet him

'Hello William, Molly will be down in a minute,' she said politely, but his brown eyes were suddenly transfixed on something above her.

When Jessie turned round a lump rose in her throat. Standing on the staircase was a beautiful vibrant woman. Molly looked so like her mother had at that age.

'Oh to be like that again.' thought Jessie 'to have the youth with all the hope and promises that went with it.'

The look in William's eyes said it all, and Jessie had to turn away to choke back a tear.

'Don't keep her out too late young William, she has a busy day in the shop tomorrow.'

'Don't worry Mr. McDermott, I'll have her back in good time.'

William reassured them both as he opened the door and they stepped out into the warm night.

After the heat of the day, a cool breeze was blowing and small goat hair like clouds streaked across the summer sky giving the evening an air of mystery. Molly talked on and on about her day in the shop with William only half listening. His eyes were taking in with wonder, her face and her hair. Beautiful perfume was filling the air. To just hold her, he thought, would be such a privilege and would be approached with the utmost reverence. He knew if he got the chance he might never let her go. There was so much he needed to tell her but he would have to wait for the right moment. It came sooner than expected when she sat down on the stone pillar at the bridge overlooking the river. With his heart thumping high in his chest he began.

'Molly ... Ahem,' he coughed, 'Molly,' he continued, 'you don't know how much I long for the school holidays, and you know why? It's because I'll be seeing you. You are in my thoughts a lot of the time and I find it hard to study. I even think about you first thing in the morning. I hope you don't mind me saying this but I must tell you how I feel.'

Taking her hand in his, he looked straight into her eyes and whispered.

'I think I love you, I have always loved you, I want to hold you close.'

The breeze blew cold on Molly's face as he suddenly held her in a very gentle embrace. She had never thought of him in this way. The emotions stirring inside her now left her speechless. Then in her shyness she managed to utter his name.

The two friends continued to embrace for a few moments, then, unsure of their new found feelings, they began to stroll slowly and silently in the direction of the dairy. As William left her side to purchase some ice cream, Molly watched him closely. She knew his words were sincere and genuine but yet in her own heart she felt there could never be anything more between them. While she did not want to hurt him, she also did not want to lose a friend. Now she felt would have to be honest with him and tell him.

'I know, I'll go and talk to Roseanne, she will know what to do.'

Molly succeeded in avoiding William for the next couple of days and as soon as Wednesday came around she wasted no time. Hopping on her bike she set off early. There was an urgency in her now to talk to her friend. On reaching the house Roseanne's mother informed her that Roseanne and Tom O' had gone to Bray for the afternoon and might not be back until later that evening. Thanking her, Molly turned disappointedly from the door. She looked worriedly up and down the street. Where would she go now?

Who could she talk to? She couldn't go back home, that was out of the question. Not really knowing what to do she turned her bike towards the coast road which J.J. and she had travelled so many times before. It was a long way to go and she was very tired when she reached the Hill of Howth. Parking her bike at the little wall, she followed the winding path along the cliffs until she reached her favourite spot. A rich carpet of green grass rolled all the way down to the waters edge. The vast blue green water stretched out below her and she felt a oneness with the cry of the seagulls as they encircled the tall lighthouse.

Sitting down on the ground, she hugged her knees up close. The events of the night with William kept going round and round in her head.

Tears threatened to fall as her eyes filled up quickly and overflowed down her cheeks. Deep inside her heart she ached for someone to talk to.

'If only Mammy was alive,' she sobbed bitterly and hugged her cold knees even tighter.

Within seconds a gentle wind rose up and encircled her form. Mystical hands fashioned from the breeze began stroking her hair in a most soothing way.

This caressing and massaging caused her neck to move slowly from side to side. Soon she fell into an almost hypnotic state of relaxation. Easing back gently on the ground the wind cushioned her movements as a deep sleep came over her. While she slept a calm descended on her soul, and the sun warmed her young body. The only evidence of what had just taken place was the gentle breeze occasionally ruffling her lovely hair.

Having slept a deep sleep for almost an hour Molly awoke to an energising refreshment which caused her to think more clearly.

Leaping to her feet with great enthusiasm she said aloud;

'I know what to do now, I'll go back and talk to William.'

She walked calmly to her bike and headed for home. It was almost dark when she got there, so she decided it would be better to call around to see William after breakfast next morning.

Maybe Jessie would not mind her being a half an hour late at the shop just this once.

CHAPTER TEN

Hattie Thornton awoke from a very restless sleep. She had taken to her bed early as she felt rather tired. But now at 3 a.m. her body was on fire. The moisture covering it was cold and she could feel a tightness in her head. Her hormones were once more waging war with one another.

How many more years must she suffer this she wondered. Turning on the light she reached for her cigarettes but found the packet empty. Reluctantly she got up and searched the drawers but with no success. How could this be? She was sure she had some. Then she remembered there was one in the ashtray in the kitchen where she had not time to smoke it earlier. Tipping gently down the stairs, she reminded herself to ask William to go to the shop first thing in the morning. As she sat smoking in the warm kitchen, the sound of the clock ticking was her only company.

'Isn't it strange, at this hour, its as if the whole world is asleep and one feels quite alone.' she observed thoughtfully,

Having no more cigarettes she got up and decided a warm bath and a change of nightdress would relax her. Eventually at 4.30 a.m. she climbed back into bed and drifted off to sleep.

Sure enough after breakfast William set off on foot to the little corner shop for a packet of 'Craven As' for his mother. But as he turned the corner he failed to see Molly approaching on her bike from the opposite direction. Parking the bike against the railings she took a deep breath, straightened her coat and proceeded slowly up the steps. She rang the bell several times and getting no answer she turned to leave. Suddenly the door opened.

'Hello Molly,' said Julie, 'what brings you here so early?'

'I've come to see William about something. Is he in?'

'Well no, he's just gone round to the shop for his Mother's cigarettes but he'll be back soon.

Come into the sitting room while you're waiting,' and she motioned to her with her hand.

"Would you like some tea?'

'No thanks, I've just had breakfast.' said Molly politely, as Julie shut the door and left her.

Gazing around the large room its sheer size seemed daunting.

On hearing voices as he came down the stairs, Seamus followed Molly into the sitting room. Opening the door He saw her gazing up in wonder at the crystal chandelier. Her expression was very beautiful. An excitement ran through him and suddenly he had an overwhelming desire to kiss her.

Taking a few steps nearer, he put his hands on her shoulders and spun her round. His mouth came clumsily down on hers as he just froze on the spot. He pulled her closer and she could feel his hard body pressing against hers.

His grip was firm and for a second she felt she might suffocate under the pressure of his lips. Slowly his hand moved up towards her breast and she struggled to pull away.

Meanwhile William, walking up the street spotted her bike leaning upright against the railings.

Quickening his steps he glanced at the open window as he fumbled with his keys. He dropped them in shock as he saw Molly and Seamus locked in a passionate embrace. Tears of betrayal welled up in his eyes and clouded his vision. He almost tripped as he turned away ran down the steps and back into the busy street. His mothers cigarettes were forgotten. Nothing mattered only that Molly had deeply upset him and with Seamus of all people.

Unaware that William had seen them, Molly was busy trying to prise herself out of Seamus's strong grip. Suddenly the wind rose up and knocked over a vase on the table behind them.

As it crashed to the floor Seamus let go of Molly as quickly as he had grabbed her and she fell down onto the Persian rug. As she struggled to get up her eyes flashed with temper.

'How could you?' she shouted at him.

'What's up with you Molly?' he asked as he picked up the glass from the floor.

In the silence that followed she realized that Seamus did not realize just what he had done.

'What's gotten into you Seamus?' she said shaking as she tried to straighten her clothes.

Holding the shattered pieces of the vase he sheepishly lowered his eyes.

'I didn't think you'd mind, I've seen how you look at me sometimes.'

'I don't know what you mean. I thought you were my friend.'

Seamus kept looking at the floor unable to face her. Maybe he should apologise but after all it was only a kiss. He could not understand why she was making such a fuss.

Unable to cope, Molly burst into tears.

'It's terrible to see you cry.' said Seamus yet unable to .comfort her. Molly ran tearfully from the room.

Just then Hattie appeared on the top of the stairs.

While wondering where William could have got to With her cigarettes, she caught sight of Molly as she ran across the hall and out through the front door.

She was just out of earshot as Hattie called loudly after her.

'Is something the matter dear?'

When Molly reached home she went for refuge to her room. Throwing herself down on the bed she gazed up at the ceiling. Wiping the tears from her eyes she thought about what had happened less than an hour ago. More deep thoughts and feelings welled up inside her. What on earth was happening? Before she had been just a person, equal to the boys and sharing in their games, but now everything was different. Now it was so obvious that she was a female. The boys were attracted to her, and unknowingly to herself she seemed to be igniting a passion in them. And there was a great element of danger in it too. From now on she would have to be careful and not encourage them in any way. Maybe she should withdraw from their company a bit and not be quite so familiar with them.

'I suppose it wasn't Seamus's fault really, after all he only wanted a kiss.' she thought.

But he should have asked her permission first, she was not there to be grabbed. A kiss should be given freely and with love. This was her first kiss, it should have been special but now everything was spoiled. She relived the incident over and over in her mind. His lips on hers, his body pressed close. It was over now but how was she going to forget about it? She could not go back to the house see William, she might run into Seamus. The whole thing was such a mess.

True to her word she took herself off on her bike every evening. Riding through the large gates of the Phoenix Park, the fields stretched out for miles ahead. Luscious green grass with large dominant trees and little hills and valleys provided a wonderful home for the deer and fawns that roamed around quite freely. The well-to-do people riding by looked ever so proud and even the horses seemed to take on an air of superiority. Molly marvelled at the wonderful creatures. Lying back on the grass she gazed upwards at the sky and she felt the presence of God looking down from the heavens. She knew that she was privileged to be part of this world He had created. The wind rustled the leaves and the sun warmed her body.

Running her hands through the velvet grass its earthy smell gave her skin a pleasant aroma as the two natural scents blended together She watched the deer suckling their young and she thought of the miracle of birth. She wondered how her mother felt when she was carrying her in her womb. Did she get the chance to hold her before she died? What was the sense of her dying? One thing Molly did know however was that she would make her mother proud of her.

As she spent many hours in solitude with nature, she grew closer to her inner self. It was times like these which helped her to realise what she wanted from life. She did not need the company of others. At this time nature was filling the void and she found peace in her heart.

Chapter Eleven

The leaves began to fall, twirl and dance along the roads. Autumn was drawing her golden cloak ever so slowly across the wonderful green colours of summer. The evenings were getting shorter and the little animals in the park had begun storing up food for the cold winter ahead. Heavy showers of rain prevented Molly from travelling and she missed her little outings. The boys letters were less frequent now and not very informative and in turn Molly's replies were of a similar nature.

On Christmas Eve she attended a crowded midnight Mass. Although feeling a little awkward she walked over and to speak with Hattie Thornton and the boys. They all shook hands and wished each other a happy Christmas. However back home it really did not feel like Christmas as she tried hard to get into the spirit of things. After a delicious dinner she was helping Jessie wash up when a knock came to the door. Roseanne and Tom O' were standing outside.

'Molly I have to talk to ya,' said Roseanne excitedly, ' can ya come out for a while?' Turning to Jessie, Molly said quietly:

'I won't be long Aunt Jessie, leave the dishes and I'll finish them when I come back.'

Jessie raised her eyebrows with relief and surrendered the dish cloth. She would not argue with that.

Once outside Roseanne almost pushed her hand into Molly's fac :

'Well, what do you think Moll?' she said smiling broadly.

Taking her hand Molly held it back a little and there on the third finger of her left hand was a ring.

Not an engagement ring however (Tom O' could not afford that just yet) but a friendship ring, the next best thing. As far as Roseanne was concerned it put a seal on their relationship. She was beaming with happiness and just could not keep her hand still. Tom O' looked on with a big smile on his face.

'Oh I do love 'er,' he said and Molly gave them both a big hug. She was so happy for her two friends. Obviously wanting to be on their own they left Molly and she returned to the dishes. She began thinking about her own life. Would she ever meet the man of her dreams. He had to be out there somewhere

'I wonder what he is doing right now,' she thought, ' Where does he live? Imagine he doesn't know me and yet we share the same world.'

If he came into her life she would give him all the love she had, of this she was quiet sure. Christmas seemed to pass quickly that year and in Contrast, the month of January passed more slowly.

At no 28 Hattie Thornton reached for an ashtray and stubbed out her cigarette in a hurry. It was high time she went shopping for some new clothes. Hurriedly she went to the phone and rang for a taxi. When it arrived she stepped into it and instructed the driver to take her to town. The shops were beckoning and Hattie always found them irresistible.

Sitting back in the seat she began to relax. This was such fun. After the dull dark colours of winter, the vibrant bright colours of the new fabrics on offer stirred up a great excitement in her.

Moving in and out of each department store, she was constantly touching and feeling the fabrics. Holding the garments next to her body, she smelt the unmistakable smell of virgin cloth. Each purchase heightened her passion until she almost screamed with delight as the shop assistant brought her 'the perfect outfit.' Hours later exhausted, happy and very fulfilled, she climbed back into the taxi with her boxes and packages filled with her purchases. The driver packed them carefully in the boot, while Hattie sat exhausted in the seat. It had been a marvellous morning shopping. Pity there was nobody to share it with. As the taxi headed for home she began thinking about Molly. It was a long time now since she saw that little girl, especially now with her two boys away. She could call to Mc Dermott's shop on the way home. She fancied a nice piece of fresh fish for her tea and she could kill two birds with the one stone.

In the shop Molly was busy carefully weighing the fish and did not notice her customer step in.

Surprised at how pale the young girl looked, Hattie enquired about her health.

'Oh I'm fine Mrs. Thornton,' she replied shyly.

'Tell me have you heard from my boys lately?'

'Yeah they write the odd letter now and again.'

Sensing something was not quite right Hattie had an idea. 'You know something' she said in a matter of fact way,

'I'm quite alone in the big house these days.

Why don't you come over for tea some afternoon my dear?'

Completely taken aback by this suggestion Molly hesitated to answer. So Hattie continued speaking without giving her a chance to reply.

'Wednesday is your half day I've heard, isn't it dear? Well I will expect you next Wednesday at 3 p.m. sharp. Now don't keep me waiting.' Then after purchasing two nice pieces of plaice, she paid Molly, took her parcel and left the shop.

Molly was in such a dither. How could she go and have tea with Mrs. Thornton. What would she talk about and even more serious what would she wear? In all the years she had known the lady she had never had a conversation with her.

Oh no! Molly Malone was not looking forward to next Wednesday at all.

CHAPTER TWELVE

Like all dreaded appointments, Wednesday came round much too quickly. Molly reluctantly headed off towards No. 28. She knew she was in plenty of time as Mrs. Thornton had insisted on her being punctual. Spring was in the air and the stately old trees were budding right across the city Daffodils planted in rows nodded approvingly to her as she sped past on her bicycle with her coat flying wide behind her. She felt a great excitement stirring. It would soon be summertime and she hoped this year would be a really good one.

Opening the gate at no.28 thoughts of the previous year's embarrassing event came back to haunt her.

'Good afternoon dear,' said a familiar voice from behind the privet hedge. Then Hattie appeared, basket in hand, full of freshly cut daffodils.

'You're just in time Molly, Julie has prepared a lovely tea for us. She has gone to visit her sister out in Dalkey so we have the whole house to ourselves. Let's go in shall we and see what treats she has in store.'

Molly offered to carry the flower basket for Hattie and the latter graciously accepted. Feeling very shy and awkward the young girl walked behind her up the granite steps and into the house. Over the years when Molly visited the twins she had only ever been as far as the hall (except for that fateful day and those moments with Seamus.)

However now on entering the kitchen she noticed it was twice the size of Aunt Jessie's. A large yellow coloured Aga cooker at the far end gave a lovely warm feeling to the room, while the aged wood of the oak cupboards suggested a cosiness of its own. Displayed on an Irish Linen tablecloth covering a large table, was a delicious array of sandwiches and a big mouthwatering chocolate cake.

'I'm afraid I don't use the dining room much when the boys are away except for the odd dinner party. The kitchen doesn't seem as lonely. So if you sit there Molly,' said Hattie pointing over to the seat next to the window, ' I'll put on the kettle and make us a nice cup of tea. How are your aunt and uncle keeping?'

'They're fine thank you Mrs. Thornton.'

'They have a nice little business going for themselves in that shop. Do you like working there?'

'Yes I do,' replied Molly not having given it much thought, 'Most of the customers are okay and I like being in charge, although sometimes it can get very cold and messy.'

'Help yourself to a sandwich,' said Hattie walking back over to the table and lifting a plate.

'Do you take milk and sugar?.'

The tea appeared a red golden colour as Hattie poured it into the beautiful delicate china cups.

'Both please.' replied Molly.

'So if you had a chance to do something different, what do you think it would be child?'

Molly thought for a moment.

'I don't know. I would love to be married, with a nice house and maybe four children.'

Looking quickly over at her, Hattie continued;

'But surely you must have thought about travelling and seeing a bit of the world first?'

Looking confidently back into Hattie's face, Molly made a very serious reply, 'I have thought a lot about what my life will be like and what I want from it. To me love seems to be the only reason that every thing exists, therefore I want to spend my life loving. If I can do this then other things are not so important.'

Struck by the sincerity of her words, Hattie thought to herself, 'This girl is a dreamer. Well I'm not going to be the one to disillusion her.

Best leave that to somebody else.' Then aloud she asked, ' What about excitement and discovering new things?' as she topped up their tea cups.

'Oh yes, I love that too, like the day I went into town with my friend Roseanne. We had such fun. It was my first time to go to town without Aunt Jessie and…'

As Molly relived her adventure Hattie was amazed to see her whole face light up. Molly's expresion of sheer innocent fun and wonder struck her to the heart and reminded her of her own youth.

Then dipping her finger childlike into the chocolate icing Molly finished her exciting tale by compplimenting Julie on her cooking.

'Why, thank you my dear, I shall pass your kind words on. Now when you're finished your tea I'll bring you on a little tour of this house, would you like that?'

'Oh yes,' said Molly as she tucked into another smaller slice of cake. All that sugar seemed to have no effect on her young figure at all observed Hattie and yet she knew that if she indulged in the same way, her waist line would get larger by the day. Still, watching the young girl enjoying the cake pleased Hattie immensely.

'Right, we'll leave the dishes as Julie usually does them before she retires.' Then, leading the way to the dining room Hattie continued, 'this house is really too big for one person you know. Only for the boys coming home on holidays I would be tempted to sell it. I always fancied a nice little house in the country.'

Looking up Molly noticed how high the ceilings were with the wonderful plaster mouldings and the matching centrepiece holding the exquisite chandelier. Hattie's eye for antique furniture and her marvellous sense of elegance could be seen everywhere. On the landing in a tall glass case was a statue of the Virgin Mary with a little light shining at her feet.

'I pray here every morning and evening' said Hattie and it brings me great comfort and peace.'

'What's up there?' Molly asked, pointing to a little door at the end of the landing.

'That's the attic dear.'

'Could we go up there?' asked Molly curiously.

'I suppose so. It's usually locked but I think the key is on a ledge above the door. I know it's a while since anyone has been up there.'

Molly followed Hattie up the stairs. Feeling around for the key Hattie smiled when she eventually found it. However when the heavy iron key refused to turn in the lock for Hattie, Molly had a go. She was delighted when it turned with a definite click. Then the heavy door creaked open and Hattie pulled the light switch. Looking around Molly felt as if she had suddenly stepped back into another time. Old clothes, lamps, and furniture vied for space in the crowded stuffy room.

Two large trunks stood in the centre, while eerie cobwebs hung everywhere. Molly could not help thinking that this room belonged in a fairytale.

'I told you it's been a long time since anyone was up here,' said Hattie, dusting off an old rocking chair. Then pointing to the trunks, Hattie told Molly that her party dresses were in one and her trousseau was in the other.

'Would you like to see them ?'she asked excitedly.

'Oh yes please,' said Molly trying to hide her own excitement. As Hattie lifted the lid off the trunk a small breeze caught the fabrics and sent a slight ripple of wind through them. Taking Molly's hand in hers Hattie asked concernedly,

'What is this mysterious breeze that my boys say follows you everywhere my child?'

'I don't know. Aunt Jessie says it's been with me ever since I was born. It seems to protect and comfort me when I need it most. I know it makes me different from others, and I find it hard to keep friends.
People don't understand me.'

'Perhaps it frightens them, have you ever thought of that? ' asked Hattie.

'Oh Mrs. Thornton, I don't know anymore. I hear the women in the shop whispering behind my back. My friend Roseanne jokes and says it could be my guardian angel.'

'Well, let's not worry about that now,' said Hattie patting her shoulder, 'come let's try on some of these dresses.'

Lifting out a brilliant yellow sequenced fabric from the top of the trunk, Hattie exclaimed;

'This was one of my favourites,' then placing it carefully on the lid she continued;

'Oh look at this blue one, I wore this to my first opera,' then dropping it too she threw her two hands up in the air and with a deep sigh said, 'and this one, I wore this special one on my first night out with dear James.'

Standing up she held the pretty chiffon dress against her older body.
Then looking at Molly she suddenly had a pleasing thought;

'Here, why don't you try it on it looks about your size?'

Molly did not hesitate. Shyly she turned her back to Hattie and began unbuttoning her blouse as Hattie continued rummaging in the trunk. A few moments later, with the dress fitting her like a glove, she released her hair and shook it free from the red ribbon that bound it.

'Well, what do you think?' she asked excitedly.

Hattie looked up and her face went pale. 'Oh my Lord,' she said, putting her two hands up to her mouth in utter surprise.

'Are you all right Mrs. Thornton? Can I get you something?' asked Molly concernedly.

'No dear, I've just had a bit of a shock, that's all.'

'Don't you like it on me? asked Molly worriedly.

'Oh it's beautiful child. It's just ... standing there you could be the daughter I never had.'

At these words large tears began to well up in her sad eyes and Molly reached over and took her hand.

'Oh but it's too late now, much too late for me.'

'Don't cry Mrs. Thornton, you will always have William and Seamus. Aunt Jessie says its all laid out what children you have anyway.' said Molly.

'Fate has nothing to do with it my girl, it was me. After I gave birth to the boys, a great change came over me. Although I loved James, somehow my fear of the pain of childbirth caused me to reject him too. After a while, James gave up and left me alone most nights. Oh Molly can you imagine what it is like to love a man and yet you are so afraid of the consequences of that very love? I never got the chance to explain it to him for he died suddenly and I have regretted it ever since. But looking at you now, standing in that dress, has brought back memories of what might have been.'

Suddenly the dresses, which only moments ago seemed so important, were now forgotten with the closeness which had drawn the older woman and the younger girl together.

'I want you to have my dresses Molly,' said Hattie impulsively as she stood up and bent down to gather them up.' They should be worn by a pretty young girl and not be locked up in this dark attic. Bring these three home with you now and I will sort out the rest tomorrow.'

Molly could not believe her ears. She also could not wait to show them to Jessie when she got home.

'Oh Mrs. Thornton, thank you so much, I will take good care of them.'

'Well it's been nice having someone to talk to,' said Hattie smiling, ' it can get pretty lonely here by times. You must come again dear and soon.'

'I'll come as often as you want, I promise.' said Molly sincerely. As the two women embraced tenderly all Molly's previous fears of their meeting vanished into thin air.

Then, with the dresses carefully packed in the basket and also tied to the carrier of her bike, Molly waved a fond goodbye. As she peddled off down the street she thought happily that it looked like it was going to be a great summer after all.

CHAPTER THIRTEEN

Aunt Jessie was busy making her delicious apple tarts in the kitchen when Molly returned.

'So you're back then. Did you have a nice time?' she inquired casually.

Molly was quite breathless with excitement. 'Oh yes, wait till I show you what I have,' she said excitedly as she lifted the large parcel up on the kitchen table.

Unwrapping it quickly, she lifted a dress out, held it up against herself, and twirling around said:

'Look Aunt Jessie, isn't it beautiful? Have you ever seen such a gorgeous dress in all your life? Mrs. Thornton is so kind, not at all like I imagined her to be. We had this wonderful tea of sandwiches and cakes and then she showed me her beautiful house. In the attic I tried on her party dresses and guess what? She gave these three to me for keeps. She has more dresses too and I'm going to visit her again.'

Swirling around the kitchen she continued breathlessly; 'Mrs. Thornton is very lonely you know and now I will be able to keep her company.'

Jessie said nothing. She kept her eyes lowered as she roughly rolled out the dough. Feelings of inadequacy rose up inside her. She had never seen Molly get so excited about anything she had ever done for her and these feelings gave way to anger and jealousy towards Mrs. Thornton.

'Is something wrong Aunt Jessie?' asked Molly.

Suddenly the rolling pin came down with a bang on the table.

'Did I hear you say lonely? Well I'll tell you what lonely is my girl. Lonely is being here from Monday to Sunday cookin', washin' and ironin' with no one to talk to day in and day out. Does anyone worry about me? Oh no. But should rich, stuck-up Mrs. Thornton who has all those fancy parties to go to, just mention the word lonely suddenly we must all feel sorry for her. Well, if you think you're goin' to waste your time over at Thornton's instead of helpin' me round here you can think again. But for your Uncle J.J you wouldn't even have a roof over your head. So get any thoughts ya might have of runnin' around to the big house right out of yer mind and help me set the table for tea.'

Molly stood flabbergasted. She never expected such a outburst of anger. She had had such a wonderful afternoon and felt so happy and now Jessie's words had wounded her deeply. 'I've done nothing wrong. I was only trying to be nice to Mrs. Thornton.' she said in her defence with tears threatening her eyes.

'And I'm going back to see her and you won't stop me.'

Then she protectively bundled up the dresses in her arms and ran upstairs.

Jessie let her go, but as she was cutting the dough around the tarts she thought:

'That Mrs. Thornton has everythin', money, a social life, and most of all children of her own. Two fine sons at that. Well she wasn't goin' to take her Molly as well.'

In Jessie's mind Molly's love was hers and she did not want to share it with anyone.

At supper, J.J. sensed there was something wrong.

Trying to make light of the quiet situation he began to tell some of his usual jokes, but he gave up when he saw there was no reaction from the two women. A little frustrated, he decided it was time to retire with his pipe and slippers.

'Best stay out it,' he thought cautiously.

Sitting toying with her spoon Jessie again asked Molly whatever happened to William. They had not seen much of him since the night he took her out.

'I hope he didn't take advantage of you, if he did I'll have words with him.'

'No Auntie, it was nothing like that,' replied Molly, toying with her food, ' they're both busy taking exams right now. Look I'm feeling tired, I think I'll go to bed.'

'Right, goodnight then,' said Jessie quietly.

There was no kiss for her tonight but to his surprise J.J got an extra hug from Molly.

Much later he climbed the stairs on his way to bed. Noticing a light under Molly's door he knocked gently and peeped in,

'Are you awake?' he whispered.

'Yes Uncle,' she replied.

He came in tip-toeing across the room.

'I can't stay long as Jess will wonder what's keeping me.' Sitting down on the bed he continued;

'I noticed there was something wrong between yourself and her tonight. What happened?'

As she told J.J. about the row, Molly started sobbing.

'Now, now, none of that. Look Moll, I've been married to your aunt for thirty odd years now and deep down she's a kind and good woman, but when you love her she expects it to be on her terms. She finds it hard to share you with anyone. So it is with us, there's no freedom in her love. If you understand that then it is easier to understand her ways. Don't be too hard on her, she means well.'

With that he made the sign of the cross on Molly's forehead and left the room. She lay in the semi darkness thinking about what he had said,

'I'll just have to visit Mrs. Thornton in secret.' she thought, ' Aunt Jessie won't know and what she doesn't know won't hurt her.'

In the next couple of days Molly and Jessie began chatting again but a slight coolness had crept into their usually warm relationship and although it was not noticeable to the customers they could still sense it in the air. Jessie took to watching her closely as she worked in the shop and the house.

She kept her very busy and Molly found she had very little time to herself. One day as Molly was parcelling up fish scraps for a little beggar girl, Jessie reached over and quickly took back a piece of mackerel she had slipped in.

'You won't help the poor by joinin' them my girl,' she said, placing it back in its original box.

Then brushing past the little girl she made her way upstairs. As soon as she was gone Molly took the fish and put it back in the parcel,

'Nor by starving them either.' she said defiantly.

CHAPTER FOURTEEN

For the next couple of weeks Molly spent two hours out of her half days around at Thorntons.

A bond of great affection forged between the two women and Hattie looked forward to her visits.

One day as they sat in the garden Hattie told Molly that her boys would not be home for the summer as they had been invited to Paris by a school chum. Being their final year in college and the exams over, they were really looking forward to the holidays in France. Hattie's garden was in full bloom and Molly loved to sit under the large white parasol at the garden table. The McDermotts did not have a garden, just a few old sheds in a yard at the back of the house. So as Molly's eyes wandered from flower to flower, the colours continued to dazzle her.

'I could sit here forever,' she said relaxing back in the chair.

'Well it's going to be a long summer, for me anyway, what with the boys away, so you're welcome to sit here as often as you like. We shall have to plan a few outings though. We could go out to Donabate and paddle in the sea. There are some lovely walks among the sand dunes and the scenery is breathtaking.'

Hattie poured out the tea and offered Molly a biscuit.

'You know I was just thinking something else too my dear,' she said seriously, ' it is high time I introduced you to Chopin, Brahms and all his friends.'

'Do they live around here?' asked Molly curiously.

Hattie chuckled to herself, 'Oh Molly, forgive me for laughing, but you are so funny sometimes. These people are composers of music, famous composers, from centuries gone by. They were inspired by God himself and their music has the power to lift us from the everyday drudgery of this life and fly them straight to the gates of heaven. The best of our Irish musicians play their works in the theatre, right here in Dublin. If you would like to go I could get us a season ticket.

'Oh I'd love to go,' said Molly excitedly.

'Well that's settled then. I shall look forward to you accompanying me. Now, what will you wear? Of course my party dresses, they would be perfect. Good thing they fit you eh? Now let me think! I can get Julie to fix your hair, she's good at that. Now, you will need some shoes. We can't very well ask Aunt Jessie for those, so I'll tell you what, next Wednesday we shall go shopping to town and you can choose a pair. Would you like that?'

Picturing in her mind every wonderful thing Mrs. Thornton was saying, Molly knew she would love it.

'Of course we will have to keep the shoes here, I don't want to upset anyone, and you can change when you come over.'

Tapping her cigarette on the silver case, Hattie seemed quite pleased with herself.

'Tell me are you looking forward to it?'

'Yes, I am,' said Molly leaning on her chin as she fought hard to come out of her daydreams.

'Well its all settled then, I'll let you know when the first concert is taking place.'

Just then their conversation was interrupted as Julie hurried from the house into the garden. William and Seamus were on the phone, calling all the way from Paris.

Jumping up quickly Hattie said excitedly: 'Oh I better take that immediately. Excuse me Molly but my two darlings need to talk with me.'

As she hurried indoors, Molly called after her, 'Please tell them I was asking for them.'

'I'll see you next Wednesday dear and don't be late. Bye.'

Molly sat on in the lovely garden for a few moments thinking to herself.

'Imagine me going to a concert. Wait till Roseanne hears this.' Then getting up she began to run towards the gate. Then had another thought:

'But don't only rich people go to concerts?'

Suddenly she felt afraid. She did not feel good enough to be mixing with the likes of them. Still being with Mrs. Thornton might give her some courage.

'That's it,' she thought happily "I will hide behind Mrs. Thornton.'

Meanwhile arriving breathless into the hall Hattie was overjoyed to hear Seamus on the telephone. He was having a marvellous time. Paris was so exciting.

'And french girls are petite and ever so pretty,' he said as he handed the phone over to William.

'Hello Mother, how are you?'

'Fine thank you William.'

'Mother, there is something I have to tell you when I get home.'

'Oh, tell me now son and don't keep me in suspense.'

'No Mother I can't. It would take too long and I'm running out of change, so I'll tell you when I see you bye.' and in an instant the phone went dead.

'Drat and bother,' said Hattie annoyingly, 'why couldn't they have got enough coins before they rang. Typical, they never thought ahead.'

As she replaced the receiver slowly she wondered what it could be that William had to tell her.

'I hope it is nothing bad,' she thought seriously as she caught sight of Molly through the window riding her bike swiftly down the street.

CHAPTER FIFTEEN

Roseanne awoke with a start. Sleep was more an escape now than a pleasure. She began to dress slowly for work. Raising her arms to fix her hair she caught sight of her worried face in the mirror.

'Oh God,' she thought nervously, 'what am I goin' to do.' Then taking a deep breath she tried to put her trouble at the back of her mind and muster up some enthusiasm for the long day ahead.

'I won't have time for breakfast Ma,' she said quietly as she entered the kitchen. Conversation was difficult and she needed to be alone. "Okay darlin', I know you won't go hungry in Bewleys. Are you meetin' Tom O' tonight?'

'Em I don't know, I will probably see him at lunch time today and then I'll know.'

Waving goodbye Roseanne hurried out the door. It was raining cats and dogs as she eventually got a seat on the bus. Like big tears, the raindrops trickled down the bus windows and her fingers idly traced each drop. Sadly however her mind, was miles away.

Back at McDermott's Fish Shop Molly was full of beans. She had an air of confidence about her which was born from thoughts of exciting days ahead. Having asked Aunt Jessie for three hours off to go see Roseanne, she too made her way to the nearest bus stop

The bus just did not seem to go fast enough as she headed into town to tell Roseanne all her news.

'1 bet she will be surprised when she hears I am going to the Theatre.'

Arriving at Bewleys a little while later she caught sight of her friend dressed in the familiar black dress and white apron of a Bewley's employee. Roseanne was busy clearing a table and Molly hurried straight over to her. She immediately started telling her all her news but Roseanne was not really listening. Instead she seemed to be miles away in thought.

'We are going into town tomorrow to buy special shoes for the concerts,' continued Molly,

Still Roseanne's worried eyes did not register any excitement and in a very catty way Molly heard her say:

'So now ya have a fairy godmother as well as a guardian angel.'

Molly was taken aback the remark was so unlike her friend.

'What's up with you Roseanne? Did I say something wrong?'

Suddenly, Roseanne burst out crying.

'Oh Molly, I think I'm pregnant.' she whispered.

Molly stood shocked and speechless.

'We can't talk here,' she said looking around at some strange staring faces. She quickly took her hand and led her out towards the toilets. In the corridor Molly asked if she was sure about her condition.

'Well, I'm eight weeks late now,' she sobbed, 'and I just don't know what to do. We were only messin' about, I wanted to wait 'til our weddin' night and now everythin' is ruined. How am I goin to tell me Ma and Da?'

Now the full extent of what Roseanne was saying slowly dawned on Molly. She knew the stigma attached to girls who got into trouble. They were called horrible names like 'slut' and 'tramp'.

Society looked on them as outcasts and when their babies were eventually born, the final insult was laid upon them by calling them 'bastards'.

How could her kind bubbly friend be thought of in this way? The very idea of it upset Molly deeply. It turned the love she and Tom O' had for each other into something dirty and disgusting...it just was not true.

'Have you told Tom O' yet?' asked Molly seriously.

'No, I'm afraid to and anyway I don't know for definite whether I am or not.' she replied sobbing.

'Well, we'll just have to go to a doctor then.' said Molly quite sensibly.

'There's a place I've heard in Mercers Hospital where I can go. They do a test and then they can tell me.'

' Okay then,' said Molly giving her friend a hug, 'I'll go with you. I'll make some excuse to get out of my trip with Mrs Thornton. Everything will be alright, you'll see, don't cry Roseanne, lots of girls have babies. If you keep crying like this you'll make yourself sick. Please stop crying.'

By now the girls were getting funny looks from the other ladies in the toilets. Roseanne gave her nose a big blow and whispered to Molly that she better get back to clearing the tables. They could talk later.

When Molly left Bewleys with a heavy heart it was such a contrast to the joy she was feeling earlier that morning. She decided there and then she would do anything to help her friend

'There is nothing she can't ask me to do to help.' she said under her breath as she made her way home

The next day she waited for Roseanne in the waiting room of Mercers Hospital. She felt very uneasy. It was as if everyone was looking at her and thinking maybe she was pregnant too.

Eventually Roseanne emerged from a white door and Molly knew immediately by the look on her face that her worst fears had just been realised. Putting her arm around Roseanne, the two friends walked in silence from the big grey building.

Chapter Sixteen

Tom O'Brien strolled confidently around Brown Thomas department store. Rubbing his hands briskly together he smiled a big satisfied smile to himself. Today marked the beginning of his fifth year in employment. He knew a vacancy had arisen in the menswear department and he was very confident that he would get the position. He always thought he was quite popular with the other staff, and his impeccable attendance record was one of strict punctuality and no absent days.

Checking his watch as he started stacking the shelves, he had to remind himself of his lunch date with Roseanne in Bewleys at two o'clock.

He preferred to take a late lunch, because by then most of the rush hour was over in Bewleys and he felt that Roseanne could relax a little.

Yes, life was good and Tom O' was feeling very pleased with himself. Strolling into the Restaurant at 2 p.m, Roseanne caught sight of him as she looked through a glass partition in the dining area. Watching closley as he sat down at his usual table she realised how familiar his movements were to her. Sliding his thin hand slickly into his pocket, he took out his gold lighter and flicked the lid to light up a cigarette. As she watched him Roseanne's thoughts were very focused on what she had to tell him. Then as she walked towards the table he rose from his seat and pulled out a chair.

After kissing her on the cheek they both sat down opposite one another.

'I need to talk to ya Tom O,' said Roseanne urgently.

'Sounds serious, hope you haven't fallen for someone else?' he replied smiling at her.

Then noticing her worried face he added, 'Only jokin, what is it? What's up?'

'I'm pregnant, ' she whispered and with that a dreadful silence fell between them. Tom O' heard her words but could not absorb them.

'Are you sure Roseanne?' he eventually managed to utter.

'Yeah, I've been to the doctor and I'm pregnant alright. I'm so afraid, I don't know what to do.'

Pulling hard on the cigarette Tom O's face went a whiter shade of pale. He now fiddled nervously with his lighter as his eyes wandered aimlessly around the room. Needing to be reassured that everything was still alright, Roseanne said worriedly;

'Say somethin' for God's sake Tom O', I'm goin' out of me mind,' and she started to cry.

Tom O' reached over and patted her hand nervously.

'Well don't start crying in here, people are watching. Look everything will be okay I tell you.

We just have to sort out a few things. Yes, that's it, we have to think what we are going to do next.' and a slight panic crept into his voice.

'Ya do love me don't ya Tom O? 'asked Roseanne, desperate to hear it confirmed.

'Of course I do,' he said ' this has been a bit of a shock that's all. I'll tell you what, go and get us two coffee's and sandwiches and I'll go to the gents. We'll talk some more when I get back.'

The two got up from the table, and as Roseanne walked towards the counter she did not see him pick up his cigarettes and lighter. Nervously he put them into his jacket pocket but in his haste to get away he dropped the lighter.

After a few moments Roseanne returned to the table with the coffee and sandwiches. She sat down at the table with her eyes pinned to the main door. After ten minutes she began to wonder where he had got to. Getting up again from the table she walked towards the door. Running up the stairs she reached the toilets and asked a gentleman coming out if he would check and see if a man called Tom O' was inside. He reappeared a few minutes later shaking his head.

'Sorry luv, only some old gent in there now.'

As Roseanne headed back down the stairs she thought that maybe unknown to her he had returned to the table. But as she entered the restaurant again she saw the table was still vacant. Standing alone in the doorway she had a good view of everyone going in and out and up and down. Her head turned this way and that, over and back, again and again, until her neck ached and her eyes were dizzy. After waiting a further twenty minutes she gave up and went back to the table.

The coffee was cold by now with the milk forming a skin on the top of each cup. The sandwiches lay were untouched. Roseanne sat down as if in a daze. A cold painful fear crept into her heart.

'Oh God, he's run out on me,' she thought.

Standing up again she automatically began to clear the table, her troubled eyes filling with tears.

Pushing his chair back in position her foot stepped on an object. Bending to pick it up her tears fell on Tom O's gold lighter. Picking it up, she held it tightly for a few moments, then slid it into her pocket. Holding her head high she made her way back into the kitchen.

Leaving work an hour earlier than usual Roseanne made her way anxiously down Grafton Street.

She stood at Weir's Jewellery shop on the comer hoping to get a glimpse of Tom O' as he left work. She searched each face as the staff left the building. Finding no luck there she went over to speak to the tall doorman as he was closing up the big black shiny doors.

'Excuse me please,' she began, ' but I was looking for Tom O' Brien. Is he workin' late?'

'No miss, if I recall he went home at lunchtime, he must have felt poorly as his overcoat is still hanging on his hook. Maybe you would like to take it to him?' With her hopes sinking fast as she turned sadly away the doorman just barely heard her say;

'No thank you.'

Walking to the bus stop it was as if she was in another world.

'I'll go out to his house, he must be home by now. There must be a reason for all this.' She thought hopefully.

An hour later she stepped off the bus and hurried up the path to his house. As she knocked on the glass door, his brother Martin suddenly opened it roughly. Seeing it was Roseanne a great dark look of smugness spread across his face. Spreading his arm out he leaned on the frame of the door as if blocking her way. Roseanne stood up on her toes straining to see past him.

'Well what brings you here?' he said sarcastically.

'I have to see Tom O' its very important,' she replied urgently.

'Really,' said Martin in a cynical voice.

'Well me girl he doesn't want to see you. He's gone away, left his good job and his home and for what? a little tramp like you who couldn't leave him alone. Well, you got what you wanted and I hope your satisfied. Just don't be coming round 'ere again,' and with that he slammed the door in her face.

The loud noise sounded so final that it jolted right through Roseanne's weary young body.

As if her last hope was gone she turned around and in a daze walked slowly down the path. She had a big decision to make and it now seemed she would have to make it completely on her own.

CHAPTER SEVENTEEN

Hattie Thornton checked her appearance in the mirror just one more time before she dismissed Julie. How she loved these shopping expeditions into town and she prepared with detail. Her collection of clothes were expensive and her jewellery just as exquisite, but when the whole ensemble was put together it had a rather eccentric look of its own which was exclusive to Hattie. Molly arrived at the front door just as the black consul taxi was pulling up.

'Climb in my dear. Time is money as my late darling husband used to say.'

Then after instructing the driver as to her destination, they both settled back comfortably in the black leather seat.

'Now we can relax a bit, we're on our way.'

'Yes Mrs. Thornton,' replied Molly.

'Now my dear, I think it's high time you stopped calling me Mrs. Thornton. I would like you to call me Hattie from now on, but only if you are comfortable doing so.'

'Alright Hattie', said Molly shyly feeling very awkward as Aunt Jessie had always told her to address her elders as Mr. or Mrs.

It was a new experience riding in a taxi and Molly felt good. So many new things were happening for her lately, things which held great promise. She did hope they would all come true.

'We won't delay this afternoon dear, we are going directly to Arnott's department store' said Hattie, as they motored towards the city centre.

Then a little later she said excitedly 'Here we are' After paying the taxi driver Hattie took Molly's arm and smiled.

'Good day Mrs. Thornton,' said each shop assistant respectfully greeting their best customer as she breezed past them. Nodding her head to each one, Hattie made her way directly to the shoe department.'

'Good day Miss Watson, I would like a pair of evening shoes for my young friend here.

Size five with a little heel will do quite nicely thank you.'

'Certainly Mrs. Thornton, please take a seat and I will bring you some samples.'

Molly could hardly see Miss Watson's face when she reappeared with the shoe boxes piled high in her arms. As she took off each lid she found herself staring at shoes which were almost too beautiful to wear.

There was a great choice of colours as they were made from fabric instead of leather. One pair in particular caught her eye. They were made of white satin with a row of diamonds stitched across the toes and a butterfly shaped from diamonds on each heel. (Of course they weren't really diamonds, just very pretty glass).

A thin strap went across her slim ankles and slipped into a silver buckle at each side. Molly walked toward the mirror and her legs looked so slim and pretty.

'Oh Hattie I love them, they're fabulous,' she said looking down at her feet.

'Are you sure they fit you alright? Walk up and down a little until I see.'

Although Molly was conscious of people watching her she made a big effort to walk tall.

'Well they seem to be fine, I can see why your heart is set on them, I must say they are lovely. Put them on my book Miss Watson and if you would be so kind as to wrap them, we will be on our way.'

The helpful assistant nodded. She put tissue paper back into each shoe before replacing it in the box. Then she put a lovely soft red cloth over them before putting on the lid.

Handing the bag to Molly she said pleasantly:

'Well may you wear and thank you very much. Good day Mrs. Thornton.'

Once on the street Molly kept bouncing in and around Hattie with excitement. She thanked her over and over and promised to take good care of the shoes. Walking along Henry Street, Hattie was telling her all about her first pair of evening shoes, when suddenly Molly caught sight of a fortune teller's stall. The signs overhead caught her eye with the words 'Let Lady Luck Tell Your Fortune' 'Lucky in Love, Lucky with Money'. Tugging at Hattie's elbow she begged,

'Can we go in Hattie? I've never had my fortune told before.'

'Well Molly that's fine for you, you are young,' replied Hattie, 'but me, well I don't have much of a future. Nothing exciting is going to happen to me at my age. I've had my innings.'

'But Hattie, it's only a bit of fun,' protested Molly ' please can we go in, you'd never know what she might tell us.'

Molly continued to coax and manoeuvre Hattie gently towards the stall. A woman of olive complexion and a deep lined face looked up as they entered. Her long black hair was tied back by a brightly coloured scarf, while two large gold earrings jangled as she moved. Beckoning with her long painted fingernails she croaked at them.

'Put a note in me palm dearie and I'll tell ya your dreams.'

Whispering in Molly's ear Hattie proposed that she would go first just to prove to her that it was all a load of nonsense. Crossing the wrinkled palm with silver, the gypsy motioned Hattie to sit down on the chair opposite her. Molly went over and stood nervously behind Hattie.

The old woman slid a black cloth from her crystal ball and gazed mysteriously into it. In the silence, an eerie atmosphere arose and could be sensed by all. Then the gypsy woman spoke.

'I see that ya've had both joy and sadness in your past, and yet ya've never been completely satisfied with your life. There's an empty space in yer big heart and only your deepest desire will fill it. Ya think ya have missed a big chance and that now it is too late for ya.' Then taking Hattie's hand in hers she began to trace her fingernail up and down her palm.

'Ah I see it all more clearly now Missus. Yer great desire is buried deep in the walls of your being and neither time or fortune can find it. But ya must believe in the impossible. There are worlds within worlds swirlin' all about ya. Yeah Missus, ya will live ta see yer desire fulfilled in the future, but it'll be at an enormous price. It'll be born out of a great sadness. Ya will grieve as if yer heart will break, and yet in yer grief life will reach out and grab yer hand. Ya'll cling to it tightly for it'll be the life line that'll bring ya back to reality.' Then turning Hattie's hands over she looked deep into her eyes and continued.

'Ya've two boys, twins I think, well they too will be touched by these events. All of ya will be united in grief, but from it will come a closer bond of love and a greater understanding of each other. The vision is fadin' now its gettin' darker, this is all I can tell ya.'

As she released Hattie's hand it hung suspended in the air until Molly gently touched Hattie's shoulder.

'The woman is finished now Hattie, I think it's my turn. Hattie rose as if in a daze from the table, and Molly took her place opposite the gypsy.

'This is a pretty young un,' thought the gypsy as Molly reached out and placed the money in her hand.

'Let's see if we can find a nice young man for ya.' she said winking and smiling through her discoloured teeth. Molly smiled shyly back at her.

Suddenly the wind rose up and encircled the tent. The canvas flapped noisily against the poles.

Frightened the gypsy looked towards the entrance almost expecting somebody to be there.

Then the light in the crystal ball flickered furiously and the curtain beads rattled noisily behind her.

A shiver ran up the gypsy's spine as she reached for Molly's coin.

'Here girl.' she said crossly, 'take yer note back I can't tell yer fortune today.'

'But why?' said Molly, 'what's wrong?'

'It's the black mood that's come over me nothin' to worry about just take your money now, that's a good girl.' Then she 'shooed' Molly away with both hands, rose from the chair and disappeared behind the tent. As quickly as it came, the wind dispersed and everything calmed down.

Hattie put her arm comfortingly around Molly's shoulder. ' Come dear I think it was the wind that frightened her. These people can be very temperamental you know. We'll call back again some other day.'

'No, I won't bother,' said Molly dissapointedly. it was stupid to come here in the first place. I thought it would be fun, but now I just want to go home.'

Hattie suddenly felt that she needed the refuge of home too as the gypsy's words disturbed her more than she had let on.

She hailed a taxi and they climbed quickly aboard.

On the short drive home both women were silent. They seemed lost in their own thoughts about the eerie events of the afternoon in Dublin City.

CHAPTER EIGHTEEN.

The ferry boat sailed calmly across the dark water towards Dublin. William and Seamus were standing up on deck leaning against the railings. It was 5 a.m. and the sun was just visible on the horizon. The wind was cold and fresh and a slight spray of sea water rose up and was carried in the wind.

'It's so stuffy below deck,' remarked Seamus looking at his watch, 'we should arrive in Dublin in about one hour.' William did not reply. Lost in thought he kept watching the vast powerful sea below him. He was thinking about his dear mother and how she would react to his news.

'God I'll miss Paris,' continued Seamus, ' you know we will have to invite Pierre over to stay with us. Mother would be thrilled to have a Frenchman staying and even though her French is quite basic, they should have some very funny conversations. You and I can show him around eh, William?'

'Good idea,' replied William. Still not really listening Seamus proceeded to light up a cigarette and the two brothers sailed home relaxing with the motion of the ship. Docking at Dun Laoghaire, they made their way down the gang-plank through the main building and out to the waiting taxis. The other passengers were hurrying to and fro to their destinations. Some obviously very glad to be home.

In the black taxi Seamus remarked on how grubby he felt and that as soon as he was home he was heading straight for a hot bath.

'Then I'm going to bed after that to get a few hours sleep. That drunk kept me awake most of the night singing and shouting. Mind you, he didn't look too great getting off the boat this morning did he? Still, serves him right. Wouldn't you wonder how a man lets himself get to that stage. It's a sheer waste of a human life, eh William?'

William started making excuses for the drunk's behaviour. Soon Seamus wished he had never mentioned the man at all as William seemed to take all these sad cases to heart. So changing the subject he began reminiscing about their summer holiday in Paris.

Hattie Thornton had seen the sun rise too. She was counting the hours until her two boys returned. When the taxi pulled up at last outside No. 28 she was standing with her arms outstretched at the front door. While William paid the fare and struggled with the luggage, Seamus bounded up the steps and with one great movement swept his Mother up in his arms and carried her into the hall.

'Oh you crazy boy put me down and go help your brother with the bags.' she said laughing.

'It's alright Mother I've got them,' said William putting the heavy cases down on the floor and rising to greet her.

'I've missed you both so much my darlings. If it wasn't for Molly I would have gone off my head.'

William's eyes lit up fondly, ' How is she Mother, how's Molly.'

'Blossoming God bless her. Now come along you two, Julie is waiting to prepare breakfast, you must be hungry?'

'I'm afraid I shall have to pass on that, Mother,' said Seamus as he headed upstairs, 'I will have something later.'

'1 hope you're not going too William,' said Hattie disappointedly, ' I want to hear all the news from Paris and especially the bit you couldn't tell me over the phone.'

Then linking arms with him she steered him quickly in the direction of the kitchen. Over the delicious bacon and eggs William told his mother and Julie all about their trip. Then he produced some french gifts from his bag. Julie was delighted with her bright red beret and excused herself to try it on. For Hattie there was exotic perfume in a bottle shaped like the Eiffel Tower. Holding it up to the light she watched the sun's rays reflect in the glass and display a chrism of colours.

'So William, what is this very important news you have to tell me? You can't keep me in suspense any longer.' said Hattie impatiently.

Looking across seriously at her William said. quietly, 'I have decided to become a priest.'

His words were like an arrow aimed straight for her heart and for a moment her eyes seemed locked on the glass bottle.

'Are you sure about this?'

'Yes Mother I am.'

'But when did you decide? You do know it is a very serious step for any young man to contemplate.'

Rising from his seat he went around the table and pulled a chair up beside her.

'Mother I have always had deep feelings about this but it was a gradual thing and so gently put upon me that now, it has become part of me. I suppose the first time I really admitted it was one hot afternoon in Paris. My pals and I were sitting on the river bank. Each fellow was saying what career he should like to follow. When my turn came I said that I'd like to be a priest. It was a bit of a relief to admit it at last. Of course my friends didn't believe me but after a while they knew I was serious about it.'

Lighting a cigarette Hattie thought for a moment and then she argued;

'But William the priesthood can be a lonely and difficult life. There is a vow of celibacy to consider and you will never know the comfort and joy of having a wife and children.'

'I know this mother and I'm sorry I will deprive you of the grandchildren you deserve.' then with a mischievous smile he added 'you'll have to look to Seamus for that.' Then taking her soft hand in his with great gentleness, he told her of the strength of his commitment.

'Mother I can try to tell you with words how much this means to me, but I am unable to convey to you the depths of my feelings. You see I don't just have a vocation as such, sometimes it doesn't even feel like a religion, I...feel it's more like a love affair with God. He is there when I go to sleep and when I wake. It is almost as if he walks with me and silently I hear Him talk to me. Often when I am at prayer I find myself in awe of His power and I am drawn to His love. Oh mother I can only tell you how His love burns in my heart and soul. When doubts crop up and they do. He just instils more trust into me and I become stronger in my commitment. And I am very happy. Things that I enjoyed before hold no interest for me now, for I know I am being called and I cannot resist. But I have made this decision freely and I want you to be happy for me.'

While William was speaking to her, Hattie noticed his eyes. They took on a wonderful expression of deep joy. Being very moved by this she rose from her chair, placed her hand on his shoulder and said quietly;

'I am going into the garden to think about what you have just said. I won't be long. Help yourself to more tea and toast.'

Then she walked calmly towards the door but once outside her legs almost gave way beneath her.

She leaned supportively on the doorpost. William's emotional words had cut her to the bone and she found her tears could no longer be restrained. She was about to lose a son. She was about to lose part of the next generation of Thornton's.

'What on earth would James have thought about this if he was alive today?' she whispered.

Then sitting down on the garden seat she reminded herself that on the other hand it was a great honour for her to have a son become a priest. She began to remember the twins christening 19 years ago now, she remembered how she had offered them back to God in thanksgiving for their safe delivery.

It now seemed He had indeed heard her prayer. Memories of William's childhood came flooding back to her as she sat in the garden. How good those precious memories were now.

After a while she rose from her seat and returned to the house. Meeting William in the hallway she took his right hand in hers and pressed her other hand ever so lovingly against his cheek.

'My darling son.' she said affectionately, 'it will be years before you are ordained. But if this is what you want to do with your life, then I want you to know you have my full blessing and support. I love you William and your happiness is of the utmost importance to me.'

Just then a familiar brotherly voice called down loudly from the landing breaking the precious moment,

'1 think I will have some breakfast after all.'

CHAPTER NINETEEN

J.J. McDermott leaned back on his chair.

'Oh,' he thought to himself, 'the pleasure of sitting in your own chair in front of a warm fire on a saturday night.'

It had been a long hard week. As he watched Molly finger-dry her hair, he could not help noticing how pretty she was becoming. Yes, she was growing into a striking young woman. After lighting his pipe he reached over and switched on the radio.

Beethoven's 'Moonlight Sonata' was playing and it was one of his favourite pieces. He closed his eyes and drifted away to the sound of the keyboard. When the music stopped it was announced that many concerts would be held soon in the Gaiety Theatre. Suddenly, Molly jumped up and, as quickly, sat back down again. J.J. opened one sleepy eye and said;

'Was it a spark Moll?'

'No, Yeah... em, no,' she said nervously.

Then turning right around she leaned on his knees and gazed up at his surprised face.

'Oh Uncle J.J.' she began, ' Mrs Thornton says she is going to bring me to those concerts just mentioned on the radio, but I'm afraid to tell Aunt Jessie. What should I do?'

J.J. couldn't help but smile to himself.

'For God's sake that's not a problem. Why, your aunt Jessie loves you and would like to see you enjoying yourself. Molly, my experience in this life is that honesty is the best policy. Even if you're afraid to tell, it is worth it not to have that little monkey of guilt sitting on yer shoulder. If, on the other hand she finds out you've been telling her lies she'll be hurt, and believe me, the bridges of trust take a long time to rebuild. Now this is what we'll do, when she comes in from the kitchen I'll say I have to go to see a man in the pub and then you two will have a chance to chat.'

Hesitantly, Molly agreed and when Jessie came into the room J.J. made good his exit. With a mischievous wink to Molly he shut the door quietly on his way out.

Jessie sat down in her own chair and took out her basket of knitting. Then she asked Molly to please turn up the radio. But Molly ignored her and began talking instead.

'I'll turn it up in a minute Auntie, I have some thing to tell you.' and she began to recall all the happenings that went on in No. 28 over the past couple of weeks finishing with the promised trips to the concerts.

'Now Auntie if you still prefer me not to go I won't. I'm sorry for telling you lies but I didn't want to hurt you or Hattie.'

'So its Hattie now is it? 'said Jessie raising her eyebrows.

'Well yeah, that's what Mrs Thornton asked me to call her.'

Noticing a hint of jealousy creeping into Jessie's voice, Molly stepped nearer to her chair and hastily added:

'You're like a mother to me auntie and nobody else could take your place.'

Jessie listened intently and felt sorry for Molly as she seemed genuinely upset. Deep down she knew she had been a bit hasty that day in the kitchen when Molly showed her the dresses. She had mulled it over in her head many times since then. She knew Mrs. Thornton could give Molly things that she could never hope to.

'Sit down Molly,' said Jessie, putting her knitting away.' I'm glad you've been honest with me, You know I had a feelin' you were sneakin' around to No. 28. but 1 knew no harm would come to ya and it gave me time to think about the situation. I suppose I was jealous of Mrs. Thornton in the beginnin' and the more I thought about it the more I realised what I had given you over the years. I gave you all my time and love and people can take these for granted as they are given silently and for no worldly gain. Even you yourself will not value these gifts until you are a mother. It was all I had to give, and I didn't mind because I loved ya. Now, if Mrs. Thornton can provide ya with other things which will help ya get on in life, well that's fine by me. You go and enjoy them.'

Then leaning over to her niece she kissed her affectionately and once again Molly felt very close to her.

'Now will you let me listen to the radio?' smiled Jessie as she picked up her knitting needles.

'Of course,' said Molly and she got up immediately and turned it back on. Then she quickly left the room and ran up the stairs. A huge wave of relief swept over her. She could not wait to tell Hattie the news at Mass tomorrow.

As the congregation came out through the large oak doors of the church the next day, into the sunshine, Molly and Jessie hung back to speak to the Thornton's. William and Seamus came over to Molly immediately.

'Hello boys,' she said, 'did you have a great time in Paris?'

'Oh yes,' said Seamus, 'it was marvellous. We took some lovely photos, I'll bring them round to the shop tomorrow and you can have a look.' Suddenly he spotted a school chum and excused himself. William stepped closer to Molly.

'Will you be home this afternoon?' he asked quietly.

'Yes I will, why?' she replied.

'I'd like to call and chat for a while.'

Curious as to his serious tone, Molly, at that moment was distracted when she caught sight of Jessie talking to Hattie.

'Okay, see you later William,' she said and walked away. It gave her a lovely feeling to watch the two women who meant so much to her, shake hands.

It also gave her a warm feeling inside and a great sense of freedom.

After dinner she kept a vigil at the hall window and sure enough at 3 o'clock as promised William crossed the street. She opened the door before he had even time to knock.

'Hello William we'll go into the kitchen because Uncle J.J. and Aunt Jessie are snoozing in the sitting room,' she whispered.

'Would you like some tea?'

'That would be nice. Thank you.'

'So, what have you come to chat about?' she asked as she put the kettle on the hob.

'1 have decided to become a priest.'

Her eyes opened almost as wide as her mouth.

'I knew it, I just knew it,' she said excitedly.' Have ya told anyone else?'

'I have told mother and most of my other friends know.'

'Oh what did your mother say?' asked Molly.

'At first she didn't understand and put up all kinds of arguments but then later on she gave me her blessing.'

'But William,' said Molly moving closer to him ' you'll make a wonderful priest.'

'Thanks,' he said shyly. 'Do you remember the night we went walking together? Well, since then I've done a lot of thinking, I don't know what was between you and Seamus and it really it is none of my business but when I saw you with him that morning in the sitting room ...' Molly did not hear the rest of the sentence, suddenly she realised that William had seen them.

'Now hang on a minute, there was nothing going on between Seamus and me. What you saw should never have happened. I gave Seamus a good telling off. God why didn't you ask me before now, I could have explained.'

'But you see,' said William, 'I was very upset too. I thought you wanted him instead of me, so I didn't pursue it. Seems to me we were all getting the wrong signals. Looking back, maybe it was all for the best as I am certain now that I have found my true calling in life.'

Molly gave William a hug and said sadly 'This means I won't see you as often from now on.'

'Now don't be silly, I'll be popping around when you least expect me and I'll always be there for you if ever you need me.'

A tear trickled down his cheek and fell on her hair as they were locked together as if in a final embrace.

Forgetting all about the tea they both said good-bye, and molly walked him to the door. Returning to the kitchen she leaned on the steel bar of the cooker. A tremendous feeling of being safe came over her. She began thinking about the concerts. She was so looking forward to going. Suddenly, a gust of wind caused the pantry door to open and Molly's eyes turned quickly. As she walked over to close it a chill crept up her spine, and she shivered. It was then that she remembered Roseanne. Poor Roseanne, Molly had forgotten to tell William that her parents had disowned her and she was now living with her Aunt Clare in Ringsend. Maybe he could help her. She was sure he would. Impulsively she ran out through the wide kitchendoor. If thought if she hurried she just might catch up with him. William heard her calling him in the distance and quickly ran back to meet her.

'What is it Molly, are you alright?'

'I'm fine.' she said breathlessly. 'It's Roseanne. She's having a baby... Tom O's baby, only he's run out on her and ...'

'Hold on a sec, you're out of breath. Let's go back to the house and you can tell me it all then,' and taking her arm he guided her back down the street.

By the time they got back home Molly had told William everything that had happened to Roseanne, and William was visibly disturbed.

'What's she going to do now?' he asked worriedly.

'She is planning on going to England to have the baby adopted. Please come round with me and see her.'

'Of course I will, we'll go straight away. But you better take your coat, its chilly out there.'

A little later when riding on the bus, she turned to William and asked worriedly, ' Do men always run from babies? I don't think it's fair.'

'I'm sure it's not the babies they run from, it's probably other things as well. I don't really know.'

The bus eventually stopped outside a row of very drab looking houses and William and Molly alighted. Looking up and down the street, no. 6 was about the best looking of them. When Molly knocked on the door it was eventually opened by a small woman in her sixties. Her hair was silver grey in tight curls which still held the imprint of each small roller. In contrast her eyebrows were a darker shade and her tiny eyes looked curiously out from behind gold rimmed glasses.

'Who are you and what do you want?' she asked sharply.

'I'm Molly, Molly Malone.'

'What Malone would that be?'

'You know J.J. McDermott's Fish Shop in the Coombe well I'm his niece.'

'Why didn't you say McDermotts.' Then looking up at William she smiled,' Who are you then?'

'I'm William Thornton Maam.'

'And who would your father be?'

'He was James Thornton but he's dead now.'

' I didn't know him, what do yeeze want with me?'

'We've come to see Roseanne please,' said Molly politely.

'What do yeeze want with her?'

'We just want to talk to her.'

'And what would yez have to talk about?'

'Just things.'

'What sort of things?'

Thinking quickly Molly piped up,

'Well it's William he's come to say goodbye, he's going off soon to be a priest.'

Clare's stern expression relaxed a little and she looked up in amazement at William again.

'Why didn't ya say that in the first place, won't you come in Father,' she said politely.

William blushed a little and said, 'But I'm not a priest yet.'

'Ah yeah but you will be,' smiled Clare as she showed them into the parlour. The room was in semi -darkness and Clare closed the door behind them. Looking around they could just make out an old couch in the corner and a few chairs. Molly walked over and strained her eyes to look at some photographs on the wall.

Then after a few moments Roseanne walked quietly into the room. Switching on the light she said defiantly;

'Auntie doesn't like waste and I don't like darkness, hello Molly... William.'

William sadly noticed how pale and thin she had grown. The mischievous light that always sparkled in her brown eyes was now dimmed. A great invisible weight seemed to be heavy on her shoulders, as her hand supported her swollen abdomen.

'William is heading off to be a priest soon. Rosy, what do you think about that?' said Molly trying to cheer her friend up.

'Oh yeah,' she replied, only half listening, and walked slowly over to a cushioned window seat. As the two girls chatted, William felt totally out of place and very awkward. Words could not solve this terrible dilemma. He felt embarrassed and completely out of his depth.

'I'm catchin' the boat on wednesday mornin' said Roseanne, 'I have the address here of a hostel where I can stay until the baby's born. Will you come with me to the boat Moll?'

'Of course I will,' said Molly as she patted her shoulder.

'It's leaving very early now, and not a word to Aunt Clare about this. I haven't told her. If she knew she would never let me go. It's best if you go now because she'll come back into the room soon. She never leaves me alone with anyone for long and we can't talk with her listenin.'

Molly gave Roseanne a big hug and William did likewise.

As they were leaving Aunt Clare reappeared in the hall.

'Well that was a short visit,' she remarked sarcastically.

'I have to get home now,' said Molly anxiously.

'Well goodbye so and you too young fella.'

'Goodbye mam,' said William politely.

Clare closed and locked the door after them and Roseanne remained seated at the window. As Clare walked back down the hall Roseanne heard her mutter to herself',

'Hmm, pity all men don't become priests. It would solve a lot of problems.'

CHAPTER TWENTY

'For the next couple of nights Roseanne's sleep was interrupted by disturbing dreams of Tom O', a baby, and England as she twisted and turned restlessly. When 5 a.m. came round it was almost a relief to get out of the bed.

In the half-light she could just make out her suitcase standing against the wall. Sitting up in the bed she pulled back the curtains a little and saw that the street outside was deserted. Good; nobody was about. When she finished dressing, she caught sight of her reflection in the mirror.

'Strange,' she thought, 'I still look the same on the outside but inside I feel I have changed so much.'

Her heart felt like stone and this in turn prevented her feeling any emotions. Any decisions she had to make from now on she would decide only with her head.

After checking that she had everything she needed for her journey, she left her bedroom and sneaked down the stairs. She did not want to wake Aunt Clare up so she gently closed the front door behind her.

Once outside in the darkness a hand suddenly touched her shoulder.

'God,' she gasped, 'William you nearly gave me a heart attack what are you doin' ere?'

'Sorry if I frightened you,' he whispered, 'But Molly is waiting for you in a taxi. We're parked a few doors down the street, didn't want to wake anyone up.'

'Oh William, I'm glad you've come,' said

Roseanne so gratefully. Taking her bag they walked arm in arm to the taxi. But it was not until she was safe locked inside the vehicle that she relaxed a little.

'Gee Moll, when did you plan this?'

'Well the taxi was William's idea, you knew I was coming any way.'

The two girls held hands tightly as they were driven to the boat, both of them unaware that this would be the last time they would ever be together.

William sat in the front and tried to avoid the taxi driver's questions about why they were catching the boat.

As they drew nearer the docks, Roseanne's eyes took on a more serious expression. She had never been outside Dublin in her life, now she was heading off to another country. It was scary. She really was a young girl who personified the saying 'Ignorance is the greatest form of courage.'

Stepping out of the taxi the cold sea morning air shocked the sleep from their tired warm faces.

Roseanne and Molly ran over to the main building while William asked the taxi driver to wait.

'There's the ticket office Molly, hold me bag 'til I go pay for mine, please.' said Roseanne. Molly was very surprised how light the bag felt in her hand.

'God love her,' she thought affectionately 'she doesn't have much in here.'

William caught up with Molly just as Roseanne was returning with her ticket. Molly winked at him and, smiling, he took a brown envelope from his pocket. Then he handed it to Roseanne.

'What's this,' she said looking surprised.

'It's just a little bit of money in case you change your mind, when you get over there, you might want to come home.'

On saying the word 'home' William had unknowingly managed to break through the impenetrable wall Roseanne had built around herself. 'Home'. Oh God, she didn't want to leave it in the first place.

All she really loved was at home. Tears ran down her cheeks. She nodded as she put the bulky envelope in her pocket and in an effort to comfort her,

Molly put her arms around her and hugged her tightly. William swallowed hard and looked down at the floor.

Then when an announcement came over the loudspeaker Roseanne and Molly moved slowly towards the barriers. With their arms still around each other. Roseanne said sincerely:

'I just want to say thanks to both of yez for what you've done for me. I won't ever forget it.'

Then as the uniformed collector took her ticket she went to turn away. But turning back suddenly she gave them one final wave and was gone.

'Oh Molly, it is so hard, isn't it?' said William sadly.

Looking up Molly saw the large grey ugly ship that was taking her friend away. Suddenly her tears gave way to anger and in her anger she blamed Tom O' and Roseanne's parents for deserting her. William tried to calm her saying:

'Molly, you can't really blame anyone in particular for what has happened. I mean, society is made up of rules. Even though they are hard to accept sometimes, without them there would be utter chaos.'

Taking her gaze from the ship, she turned to him and with her eyes black and flashing she said angrily,

'Ah feck it William, society is made up of families and where are the families now?'

CHAPTER TWENTY ONE

Six months later McDermott's shop was a bustling hive of activity. J.J. had decided it was time the premises had a fresh coat of paint. Molly was busy moving the fish about to accommodate the painters, when suddenly feeling tired she decided to take a break from it all.

Sitting on the crates outside the shop the last of the summer sun felt warm on her face. She spotted Seamus strolling up the street towards her and wondered what he could want this early in the morning as he did not usually rise until well after ten.

'Hello Molly', he said politely. 'You're up early.'

'Yes because Mother sent me round to ask you if you would like to come to our house tonight. She is having a little send-off for William and myself. Nothing big, just the family. It's at six tonight so do you think you'll be able to come?'

Yeah, I will thanks,' she replied 'but I wish you'd told me yesterday. I don't suppose Jessie will mind me slipping away early. I mean look at the state of the shop, nobody will want to come in and buy fish today. It's such a mess.'

'Right, I'll see you later, bye Molly.'

'Bye Seamus.'

Arriving at Thorntons at 6 p.m. Julie greeted Molly and showed her into the sitting room.

William and Seamus were sitting by the window chatting over glasses of wine. They stood up when she entered the room and before she could protest they had placed a glass of burgundy in her hand. Awkwardly she raised the glass to her lips, and the wine tasted bitter-sweet to her inexperienced palate. She decided not to make a fuss and try make her first glass last all night.

'Come over here and look at our photographs,' invited Seamus and Molly went over and sat down between them. She could not help but marvel at the wonderful structures of the Eiffel Tower, the Notre Dame Cathedral and the Arc de Triumphe. Seamus kept skipping over some photos of pretty girls and when she brought it to his attention he just smiled and said that they were friends of Pierre's.

'The photos are lovely, I'd love to go there someday,' said Molly. 'Where's your Mother?'

'She's is in the kitchen driving Julie up the walls,' said Seamus, laughing 'Julie hates any-one hovering around her when she is cooking, and Mother, well, you know Mother, she just loves giving advice.'

Just then Hattie breezed into the room with a glass of sherry in one hand and a cigarette in the other. Molly noticed that she was a little unsteady on her feet and was smiling broadly.

'Lovely to see you my dear,' she said 'going over and kissing the young girl on the cheek.

'I must say, you are looking wonderful. Isn't she boys?'

Looking at Molly's happy blushing face, William could see no trace of that tearful girl who stood at the dock in Dun Laoghaire on Wednesday morning. Tonight her beautiful face had a special radiance about it.

'Julie has told me to announce that dinner is served, so we shall all adjourn to the dining room,' said Hattie leading the way. 'She will be joining us at the table tonight, as this is a very special occasion.'

Walking towards the dining room Molly noticed how much younger and different Julie looked without her apron.

Once in the dining room Molly realised that only in pictures had she ever seen a table laid out such as this one. The crystal glasses and cutlery shimmered in the candlelight and the flowers arranged in the centre of the table were breathtakingly beautiful. Hattie sat at the top of the table with one son on either side.

Molly sat opposite Julie and beside William. Looking down at her place setting, Molly noticed that there was a lot of cutlery to contend with. Which one would she pick up first? She hesitated.

'I know, I'll watch Hattie and do what she does.' she said cleverly.

William stood up to say grace and everyone joined their hands and bowed their heads.

'Bless us Oh Lord and these our gifts, which from thy bounty we are about to receive, through Christ our Lord, Amen.'

Hattie picked up the first fork on her left hand side and Molly did likewise, and so she continued to do so throughout the meal.

Leg of lamb, followed delicious asparagus soup and by the time the dessert was served Julie was revelling in the praises heaped upon her for her delicious sauces in the cooking.

Hattie requested everybody to raise their glasses in a toast to William on his vocation at Maynooth and Seamus in his studies of medicine at Trinity.

The strong red wine had started to take effect and Hattie was getting very emotional indeed.

'My boys,' she began her speech, ' have been together since birth, they sat side by side all through primary school and again in Belvedere College. Now it seems they are going their separate ways.' She was getting visibly upset when William rose from his seat to comfort her.

'No, I'm alright dear,' she said trying to compose herself. Then raising her glass she turned towards Molly and continued:

'I really had no idea how much you Molly, have been a part of my sons childhood until tonight. Listening to all the stories of what you got up to, It is lovely to know that you have memories such as these to look back on. Molly, you are always welcome in my house and I hope your friendship continues with this family no matter what may be.

Then raising her glass she said proudly:

'A toast... to Molly.'

Molly blushed, and for once felt that she really belonged in the big house.

'You know,' continued Hattie, 'It has been hard for me to keep going through the years without my beloved James at my side. But I think, should he be here tonight, there would be no prouder man in all of Ireland.'

The tears started to fall at this point and William took his Mother's hand and held it tightly.

Patting his hand she slowly withdrew hers and repeated again:

'I'm alright.' then taking another sip of wine she turned her attention to Julie.

'I want to say a special 'thank-you' tonight to Julie for her friendship and loyalty to me, but more important for being here for the boys down through the years when I could not. Thank you.

'To Julie.'

Everyone raised their glasses and Julie smiled bashfully . She wiped a little tear from her eye and Seamus leaned over and gave her a kiss.

'Will I serve the coffee now Hattie?' she whispered hoping to seek refuge in the kitchen to compose herself.

'Yes dear in a moment but before the coffee arrives I have just one more thing to say,' said Hattie, looking at her two boys adoringly;

'I love you boys and I wish you the world and everything good that is in it.'

'Here, here,' shouted Julie and everyone clapped.

By the time Julie returned with the coffee Hattie was winding down. For the next two hours they reminisced and laughed and told yarns and jokes. Hattie leaned back in her chair and took the special atmosphere of the night to her heart

She really enjoyed listening to that part of their lives that would never return again, their childhood.

Then catching sight of the clock she decided it was time to retire as Seamus and William had an early start in the morning.

It was late and she advised Molly to leave her bike and asked the boys to accompany her home.

Hattie and Julie stood in the doorway and watched the three young people laughing and giggling as they walked down the street.

'It's just like old times,' said Hattie, 'when they were at school together.'

'I want to thank you for a lovely evening Hattie and those kind words you said about me,' interrupted Julie.

'Taken aback by the unassuming voice of her housekeeper Hattie turned to her friend of twenty one years, and from the bottom of her grateful heart said sincerely,

'Oh no Julie, tonight it is me who is saying 'thank you' to you.' The two old friends embraced fondly and then went back indoors linking each other, and the door of no 28 closed ever so gently behind them.

CHAPTER TWENTY TWO

When Julie popped into the shop on Monday morning she found Molly looking a bit down in herself.

Placing her shopping bag on the floor she enquired,

'Well well, what's this sad face for then?'

'Oh hello Julie, I didn't see you come in I've just had a letter from Roseanne and I do wish she wasn't so far away.'

'There's nothing wrong is there?'

'Would you read her letter and tell me what you think?'

Julie sat down on the old wooden stool, took out her glasses and read the following;

Green Close,
Hatch Lane,
Liverpool,
England.

Dear Molly,

I hope you are well. The journey over was a bit rough with some of the people being sick and some drunk. I kept meself to meself but then a woman from Kildare got nosy and started askin' too many questions, so I got up and moved to another seat. I was glad to get off at Liverpool.

The hostel where I'm stayin' isn't bad and the people who run it are kind, but its not home I miss home Molly, but I won't be comin' back.

I can't forget what they done to me. It was awful when Tom O'ran out but it was worse when Mammy and Daddy put me out too. Well they can all go to hell for all I care. I'm going ahead with the adoption and when its all over I'll show them. I'll get a job and I'll be okay. Maybe you would come visit me when I'm settled. I'd love that. Tell William thanks for all he done and Molly your still me best pal.

God Bless
love Roseanne.

Removing her glasses she rubbed her eyes and handed the letter back to Molly. Julie thought to herself that it was an unfortunate situation indeed.

'Look Molly the people in these hostels are trained to deal with this sort of situation. I'm sure there is nothing to worry about. She will be well looked after.'

'I suppose so Julie,' said Molly not entirely convinced ' but I really think she hates her parents.'

' It probably only seems like that now, but in time they'll come round and take her back. Remember them that burns their bum must sit on the blister.'

Molly still did not look happy as she slid the letter into her pocket.

'Now, forget about that letter for a minute,' said Julie on a happier note, 'ask me why I'm here.'

'To buy fish I suppose.'

'Guessed wrong, go again.'

'Oh Julie I'm not in the humour of riddles, tell me.'

'Well the mistress sent me round to tell you that your off to the Gaiety Theatre on Sunday Night.'

'This Sunday?' asked Molly, her surprised eyes opening wide.

'The very one.'

'Oh I don't believe it,' said Molly excitedly and a big smile spread across her unhappy face.

'Now you must be over by four as I have to fix your hair, and you must tell your aunt Jessie in time.'

'Oh I will Julie, I promise.'

'Now seen as I'm here it would be a shame not to buy some of those tasty fillets of plaice. Wrap up four for me, that's a good girl and I'll be on my way.'

'I don't believe it. This Sunday', Molly kept repeating as she wrapped up the fish in some paper.

'That should keep her mind off that letter for a bit,' thought Julie to herself as she said goodbye and left the shop.

Although Molly had told Jessie about going to the theatre she was still a bit nervous about telling her that she would be getting dressed in Hattie's house. When she heard she asked in a sarcastic voice 'What's wrong with getting dressed here?'

'Well Julie is putting my hair up in a special way. Its so thick I can't manage it myself.'

'Hmn I see, well alright,' she said as some of the old tension returned.

On Sunday afternoon Molly could be found around at No. 28 soaking in Hattie's big iron bath. She had forgotten all about the time until Julie knocked urgently on the door.

'Hurry Molly! I have to do your hair yet.'

Molly jumped out of the water and wrapped herself in a large bath towel. She found it hard to sit still at Hattie's dressing table as Julie pressed,what seemed like hundreds of hair pins into position. Eventually, when they were both dressed Hattie and Molly stood side by side looking into the large mahogany Cheval mirror in the bedroom.

'You know something, we could almost pass for sisters,' said Hattie proudly.

Julie had to turn away to hide her smile at such a ridiculous remark. Catching sight of her in the mirror Hattie said sharply; 'Thank you Julie, as usual you have exceeded yourself.'

Just before they stepped into the taxi Molly asked Hattie if the driver could stop at her house.

'I would to love show Aunt Jessie my hair. I'll only be a minute I promise.' she pleaded.

'Oh alright,' agreed Hattie 'but you must not delay, I like to be in my seat before the performance starts.'

When the taxi pulled up outside McDermotts, Molly alighted carefully and tip-toed into the house hoping to surprise her two guardians. On opening the sitting room door she saw Jessie turn quickly. In the firelight Molly appeared as she had never been seen before.

Hattie's jewels twinkled like stars in her ears and her hair was piled high on top of her head in numerous curls. Her necklace reflected the golden colour of her taffeta dress and it shimmered as she moved. On her feet were the most beautiful shoes Jessie had ever seen.

'I thought it was royalty come to visit,' said J.J. lowering his paper and peering up at Molly from over his glasses. Standing up from the other armchair Jessie was speechless,

'I wanted you to see me before I left, do ya like it? ' she asked almost begging the right answer with her eyes

'We certainly do, don't we J.J?'

'Aye, you look like a proper princess,' her uncle said smiling.

'I have to go now, Hattie's waiting in the taxi,' and she turned for the door.

'Thanks for comin' to show me,' whispered Jessie 'I really appreciate it.'

Molly kissed her cheek and with a wave she was gone. Jessie shut the door behind her and returned to the sitting room. Picking up her needles and her wool she resumed her knitting.

'You know somethin' J.J? she said thoughtfully. 'When Molly gets dressed up like that she looks like she comes from a very good family.'

From behind his newspaper J.J. smiled to himself.

'Aye she does, a very good family indeed!'

CHAPTER TWENTY THREE

Standing outside the Gaiety Theatre, Molly looked up at the building towering above her.

Handsome couples linked together with smiling faces made their way towards the large mahogany doors. An air of excitement was everywhere. Stepping into the foyer, Hattie pointed out wonderful carvings and furnishings. Molly was only half listening. She was watching the people weave to and fro before her eyes. They all looked so beautiful and so clean. The women were elegant and the men, although not all handsome were certainly well turned out. Friends came up to greet Hattie. Shaking her hand they smiled kindly at Molly. Looking up, her attention was drawn to the staircase. It was so inviting that she felt she could walk up and down it all night. Then a young boy selling programmes interrupted her thoughts.

Hattie rooted in her purse and purchased two and she handed one to Molly, it read:

THE RADIO SYMPHONY ORCHESTRA
PRESENTS. GAIETY THEATRE 1956
Vaughan Williams: Overture, "The Wasps".
Beethoven: Violin Concerto.
Schubert: Symphony No 8
Morean: In the mountain country.
Antonio Brosa, violin.
Conductor Milan Hovart.

Walking up the stairs behind Hattie and an old friend Molly constantly looked down at her shoes. They felt just right as she stepped on the rich deep carpet. The usherette showed them to their seats on the third balcony where they had a wonderful view of the whole auditorium.

They watched all the people talking quietly amongst themselves. Then as the lights were dimmed and the curtain rose slowly a great hush came over the audience. Molly could feel her excitement rise as she waited for the unexpected.

When the orchestra began playing she suddenly felt a great surge of sound go through her. She had often heard such music on J.J's wireless at home, but it was interrupted from time to time with crackling and buzzing. Tonight, the sound was different. It came alive in her presence and she was lost in its power as she watched the orchestra.

She marvelled at how some musicians played different instruments and yet when they were all put together it blended into one fabulous piece.

While the Radio Eireann orchestra continued to weave its musical spell, Molly dreamed dreams and found a depth in her soul that she did not know existed.

When the lights went up at the interval they only proved to be an unwelcome distraction. Hattie insisted she accompany her to the toilet and Molly was reluctant to go. She didn't want to leave the magic atmosphere of the auditorium but she went anyway.

'Well, what do you think of it now my dear?' said Hattie as they queued with the other ladies

'I think its more than I'd ever imagined, 'she replied excitedly, 'I can't believe I'm here.'

The interval was over by the time they returned to their seats and Molly couldn't wait for the music to begin again. During a particularly moving piece Hattie watched Molly closely. She searched her youthful face wanting desperately to recapture in Molly what she herself had felt the first time James brought her to the theatre. Then she saw Molly's eyes fill up with tears as the music caused emotions to well up inside her. Hattie smiled and looked back at the stage. As the evening wore on Molly continued to get lost in the music. She wished she had the whole place to herself then she could really let her feelings out. She felt she couldn't share this with strangers. When the lights went up to a standing ovation she clapped until her hands went numb. She hoped, as she looked around, that nobody would notice her vulnerability. Then they sat down again and waited until most of the crowd had left, trying to hang on to the atmosphere.

Walking back down the stairs beside Hattie all feelings of inadequacy had vanished as Molly was still in awe of the music.

Outside people were rushing about trying to make their way home.

There seemed to be a magic on the streets carried out from the theatre by the delighted audience.

'Well my dear I must say I enjoyed that immensely,' said Hattie adjusting her cream gloves.

Molly looked longingly back at the rich warm glow of the theatre.

She felt she had her feet in two worlds and she knew in her heart that she could quite easily make either of them her home.

CHAPTER TWENTY FOUR

Three years later in the summer of her twentieth year Molly's physical beauty had peaked.

She stood five foot six inches tall and was likened to a fruit ready for picking. Her figure was more curvaceous than slim and her hair was still that wonderful colour it had been in childhood. Her teeth were set straight and white and even. Her smile lit up her eyes drawing the onlooker into pools of beauty. Her neck was long and slender and her face small.

To those who knew her, Molly appeared a pretty enough young girl. People spoke of her kindness and respect for her elders. But underneath these observations lay a personality capable of immense depth of feeling. Although she had been through the tragedy of her friend's pregnancy and knew the hard facts of life, she had an air of innocence about her. She had led a pretty sheltered life but her mind was very much alert and constantly seeking out truths. She knew right from wrong and sometimes it was as if she could die for her convictions. She was a good girl but she was no saint. Jessie and J.J. could both swear to that. Her mischievous ways were well known to them. Her fascination with nature kept her aloof from materialism and she seemed to be content with very little.

She knew her place and her work in the fish shop kept her humble. Although she had great energy, by evening, when it was spent, she wilted like a summer flower. However, it would take someone who really loved her to discover Molly's true womanhood. It was likened to an underground spring which moved and flowed beneath the earth. Only by being explored could she come to life fully, and love and give the joy for which she was created.

This would take a very special man indeed. In Molly's dreams he was tall and broadshouldered, but of no particular image. He would not be rough or insensitive, he would not be cruel or selfish.

Upon meeting him it would be his spirit of love she would be instinctively drawn to. He would be a kindred spirit. Oh how she ached to be held by him, to be kissed by him, to lie in his arms and hide like a little child, and then again to be taken up and carried to a place of loving. There they would reach such heights of passion that together they would be consumed by a burning fire of sheer love.

It was into such wonderful thoughts as these that Hattie interrupted. She talked on and on about William as the two women travelled the road towards the town of Maynooth. Having completed his B.A. in Clonliffe, William had transferred to Maynooth College to study for his Bachelor of Divinity degree. On Wednesdays visitors were permitted at the college and Molly was delighted when Hattie invited her along. As they drove through the college gates the haunting ruins of the old castle stood on their right, with the Protestant church just as impressive on their left. When the driver stopped to enquire from the groundsman as to which place to park, Molly suddenly spotted William standing with some friends on the left hand side of the main building. Stepping out of the car, the two women walked slowly towards him as he came to meet them. Molly was taken aback when she saw him dressed in the long black soutane and little white collar. The outfit instantly recognizable as that of a Roman Catholic priest. She couldn't understand why she suddenly felt humble in his presence.

Even his mother greeted him with a slight awkwardness, not sure if it was okay to hug him in his clerical attire.

'Hello Mother,' he said smiling, 'and Molly too, this is a surprise.'

'My darling son, how are you? I must say I didn't expect this quite so soon,' and she looked up and down at his soutane.

'We are given these the first day here Mother, I'm not comfortable in it either,' said William, and he kissed them both. Then linking their arms he guided them under the arch and into a beautiful square garden. Triangular lawns created a network of paths on which to stroll and the trees provided shelter.

'This is St. Joseph's square, I'm afraid it is the only place we can be together. The regime here is very strict.'

'Oh,' said Hattie indignantly, I was hoping to see a lot more of the place and especially your sleeping quarters. I hope they are adequate.'

'I'm afraid rules are rules here Mother.'

'Well in which building do you sleep?'

William pointed up and across at the long building on the right.

'That is where I sleep, see, the third window on the right. That is called the 'new house' it replaced the old one which was burnt down some time ago.'

Then turning to Molly, William asked curiously:

'What do you think of the place, Molly?'

'God William,' she replied looking around in amazement, its all so very big.'

William could not help laughing at this. ' Well it is a little bigger than the fish shop alright.'

'Oh that reminds me,' said Hattie, 'Julie has packed a delicious basket of home cooked food, its in the car. She also sends you her love.'

'Sorry, Mother we are not allowed accept food parcels.'

'Nonsense you look like you could do with a decent meal. Who is your superior? Perhaps I shall talk to him.'

'Oh no Mother,' said William anxiously.

'There is a strict code of rules here and it's better not to draw unnecessary attention to oneself.'

'How long will you be here?' asked Molly sounding a little worried.

'Four years Molly, I have to study theology.'

'Is that dogmatic or moral theology?' enquired Hattie.

'Both actually, then please God I will have my degree and be ordained.'

Looking around at the other students with their families Hattie asked William if he had made any new friends.

'There must be some boys here from good families,' she said hopefully as they sat down on a wooden bench under a tree.

'Special friendships are not encouraged so we stay in small groups. Anyway we only have a half hour in the whole day to have a conversation so there is not much time to make friends. On the other hand there is good fraternity between the students.'

'Do you like it here William?' asked Molly curiously.

'Well it's a lot different than I would have imagined. There is a great distance between the professors and students. The professors can be very stern. They don't like to be questioned and any kind of controversy is discouraged. There is absolutely no affection in their day to day contact with us. Most of the lads live in fear of the rules. Sometimes it feels as if we are in prison.'

'Oh my dear boy, I had no idea. We will have to see about this,' said Hattie as she lit her cigarette and pulled vigorously on it.

Turning to his Mother William took her hand gently but firmly:

'No Mother,' he said ' I came here to serve God. I knew it wouldn't be easy. But my vocation will get me through because it is deep and true. Sometimes I feel that my professors are so caught up in rules that they have lost sight of the heart of God. When I leave here I want to be different. I need them to teach me the discipline but I'll try not to lose love in the process.'

'Well I hope so William, although it may take some doing in a place like this.' said Hattie as she looked at her surroundings. 'Now tell me son, have you heard from your brother at all?'

'Yes, Seamus writes whenever the humour takes him. He seems to be having a lot more fun than I am, especially now that he is working on the wards.'

'I hope he's behaving himself and not making free with the nurses.' said Hattie anxiously.

William and Molly looked at each other and laughed. They could just imagine Seamus up to his old tricks.

It was lovely to sit in the lovely garden and chat about old times. Hattie enjoyed listening to the two young people making plans for their futures.

Then a bell rang out in the distance.

'Oh I'm sorry but I'll have to go now, visiting hours are over.'

'So soon?' asked Hattie looking at her watch.

William offered her his hand and she rose from her seat. Walking back slowly towards the arch, the sound of the stones crunching under their feet broke the sad atmosphere which had descended on the little party.

On reaching the car Hattie turned to William and said,

'At least let me give you this money,' and she pulled a small envelope from her bag.

'But Mother, what do I want with it, what have I to get? I have no need of money here. The only thing I can accept is some underclothes.'

Suddenly Hattie began to realise how useless material things were in a place like this.

Noticing her disappointment William leaned forward and kissed her on the cheek.

'Don't be worrying I have everything I need. Now you take care of yourself and come again soon. I look forward to your visits.'

Hattie gave him a big hug and then turned rather sadly and got into the car.

'Thanks for coming Molly and won't you look after Mother for me.'

'Yes I will ,' she said sincerely and she gently brushed her check against his.

As they drove away she waved and waved at him through the back window. Hattie wiped the tears from her eyes with her lace handkerchief and said in a rather shaky voice;

'Oh Molly, I hope that the people will appreciate what my son is sacrificing in order to serve God.'

CHAPTER TWENTY FIVE

By 8th of February 1956 Molly's concert-going had begun in earnest and the range of music to which she was exposed to was quite extraordinary. Once in the theatre, it was as if she was in another world far removed from the fish shop. But she never took it for granted. Instead her appreciation was evident, as daily, in thanks for Hatties gifts, she gave more of herself to the people she served.

Hattie and Molly had taken to arriving early at the theatre as this allowed them more time to chat with friends in the foyer. Hattie's friends would gather around Molly and enquire as to how William and Seamus were doing in their studies. They always made her feel at ease and she would blush when they commented on her youth and beauty.

It was on such an occasion as this, when looking around the foyer at some familiar faces, that Molly suddenly spotted one tall young man who stood out from the crowd. Chatting away to an elderly couple she noticed a boyish grin appear from time to time on his handsome face. Feeling an instant attraction she watched him closely for a few moments. Then she nearly died with embarrassment when he turned his head and caught her stare. She blushed and quickly looked away. His gaze returned to his companions, but in an instant he had turned back again. Molly saw a big smile spread across his face as he bounded over in her direction. Suddenly, she panicked and side-stepped in behind Hattie. As he drew nearer she was more than surprised to hear him say;

'Hello, Auntie Hattie.'

Before Hattie could respond he had taken her hand and, raising it to his lips, gently kissed it. Hattie looked up in a temporary state of confusion. Then she gasped;

'My dear boy, I hardly knew you. My how tall you have grown and how elegant you look. What have you been doing with yourself?'

Molly smiled at him as he tried to get a word in edgeways, but that was impossible as Hattie continued with her questions.

'Tell me now, how is everyone down at Riversdale House? My big brother and your handsome one? Are they well? and what of Doireann? I hope she is behaving herself?'

The young man laughed.

'They are all very well Aunt Hattie.' and he continued staring at Molly. She blushed even deeper as a shiver of excitement ran through her. Unable to look away, she found herself falling into his wonderful brown eyes. Noticing what was happening between the young people Hattie turned and taking Molly's arm she said delightedly:

'I don't believe you have met my companion,
David Furlong, I would like you to meet Miss Molly Malone.'

Molly stepped forward a little and shyly held out her hand. David reached for it without taking his eyes from her face. Molly's eyes sparkled in response but neither of them said a word.

Smiling mischievously Hattie excused herself and turned back to talk to her friends.

'So Molly, how come you are here with my Aunt Hattie? I never thought that she would have such a young companion.' asked David curiously.

'Well,' explained Molly, ' I went to school with William and Seamus and I'm still friends with them. But when they went away Hattie asked me if I would visit her. I think she was lonely in the house so I started going round on my half day from the shop. I'm very fond of her and she's been good to me.'

As if afraid that a pause in the conversation might separate them, Molly kept on chatting nervously. David did not even try to interrupt but just stood there watching her, getting lost in her beauty and charm.

Then Hattie interrupted and requested David to escort them to their seats. Linking his arm up the stairs Molly was sure he could feel her trembling at his closeness as she tried to stay calm.

When they reached their seats David suggested, to Molly's delight, that he rejoin them at the interval. During one of her favourite pieces, 'Ravel's concerto' Molly found her concentration wandering as her eyes kept searching the auditorium for a glimpse of David. Then it suddenly dawned on her that maybe he was looking down from a higher balcony. How her heart swelled at the thought of it.

When the interval came an hour later, Molly was very impatient with the crowd. They seemed to be moving slower than usual towards the foyer. She ducked and weaved through them as she hurried down the stairs. Finally, on reaching the last step, she saw him patiently waiting below.

With friends coming over to chat to them they did not have much time to be alone, but Molly knew by the way he kept stealing glances at her that something very special was happening between them. He took every opportunity to touch her which made her feel safe and protected.

Hattie rejoined them and David exaggerated his movements as he offered his arms in a mock gesture for the second time. They laughed and were only too willing to accept. Taking their seats they promised to meet up again at the end of the performance.

During the second half Molly found herself wishing David was sitting beside her. She needed to share the music, oh how she wanted to share the music with him.

Then when the performance was over they left the theatre together. David whispered in her ear:

'Could I call round to the shop tomorrow?'

'Oh yes do please,' she replied and suddenly the night took on an even more magical feeling.

'Now my dear boy you must not forget and call round to see me too, do you hear?' insisted Hattie kissing him goodbye.

'Oh I will Aunt Hattie,' he promised, looking straight across at Molly.

On reaching home Molly did not delay but said a quick goodnight to everyone and hurried to her room. She needed to be alone to bring back the wonder of the evening. She lay on the bed and it seemed as if she could almost make David appear by just thinking about him. His attractive smile drifted into her minds eye. Many boys had often flirted with her before, mostly in the shop, but there was something special about David. His very presence excited her. She jumped off the double bed and looked at her reflection in the mirror. Her eyes wandered over her body and back to her face. She tried to see herself through his eyes. Was he pleased with her appearance? she wondered. Oh she hoped he was.

She got undressed and put on her cotton nightdress. Wandering over towards the window she pulled back the lace curtains and looked up at the stars. Tomorrow she would see him again.

Then she climbed back into bed but was still too excited to sleep. Eventually after much turning and twisting her eyes grew heavy and clutching the pillow close to her body Molly drifted into a wonderful sleep.

CHAPTER TWENTY SIX

Molly woke just as excitedly the next morning, suddenly remembering the night before. She lay in bed thinking to herself that this was it. He was definitely the man of her dreams. While dressing she was aware that her working clothes did not measure up to her dress of the previous evening.

All morning she kept nervously watching the window but there was no sign of him. He could not have forgotten. Maybe she should have written the address down. After lunch things looked no better until just around 4 p.m. she noticed a motor-bike parked outside.

Then David walked briskly into the shop. His thick black hair which was slicked back neatly the night before now hung tousled on his forehead and he flicked his fringe back in a most attractive way.

'Hello Molly,' he said smiling as he approached the counter.

'Hello,' she said shyly realizing that they were now alone.

'Did you enjoy last night.?'

'Oh yes, everything was lovely,' she replied as she fingered her hair nervously.

'You know something, I couldn't get over how well Aunt Hattie looked. I think she's getting younger.' Molly giggled.

Then looking her up and down David remarked, 'You look as good in that apron as you did in your lovely dress last night.'

Molly looked down at her apron and smiled in a flirty sort of way.

'You're not used to getting compliments, are you,' he said taking her by the hand. She just wished he would stop embarrassing her and talk more meaningful.

'Is that your motor bike,' she asked trying to change the subject.

'Yes, I've had it two years now and its great round the city.'

'What do you work at David.?'

'I'm an electrician by trade.'

'But I don't understand, Hattie told me you were a Wexford farmer.'

'Did she now, and which would you like me to be?'

'Oh I don't know,' she answered blushing.

Completely taken by her reaction David asked quickly,'

'Tell me Molly do you like dancing?'

'Yes I do.'

'Would you like to come dancing with me?'

'Oh yes but I can't dance very well.'

David laughed.'Neither can I but shur we can teach one another.'

Then glancing at his watch he continued:

'I'll have to go back to work now, but I could pick you up on Saturday night. Would that be okay?'

'What time?'

'About half eight.'

'That's fine.'

'Bye till then.'

'Bye David.'

'Goodbye Molly.' he said as he let her hand go.

As he left the shop she watched him through the window. Confidently he kicked-started the bike, revved the engine and sped off down the street.

By Saturday Jessie McDermott was a worried lady. 'I don't like the idea at all of you going around on the back of a motor-bike.' she said

'And you better take my big coat with you.'

Molly looked down at the rather dowdy coat.

'No I'll be fine honest, don't be fussing.' She said as she opened the door to David's knock.' Hello David. Aunt Jessie, I'd like you to meet David Furlong.'

'How do you do,' said David politely as he shook her hand.

'Is that your van outside?' asked Molly, 'unable to see the bike anywhere.'

'I only borrowed it. I can't very well bring you to a dance on the back of a bike, now could I Mrs. McDermott?'

A look of relief spread across Jessie's face.

'I won't be needing this coat now thanks,' said

Molly and handed it back to Jessie.

'Well just make sure your home early, you know how your uncle worries. He likes you to be in at a respectable hour.'

'I promise,' said Molly stepping out into the dark street.

'Goodnight Mrs. McDermott.'

'Goodnight David.'

It was Molly's first time in the Crystal ballroom. The eight-piece band looked so smart in their black tuxedos and matching bows. In the centre of the ceiling above them a large revolving crystal with reflecting mirrors bounced the lights off the surrounding walls. The strong quick beat of the drums set up a vibration in the floor causing a tingling sensation in the back of Molly's legs, and she immediately wanted to dance.

The first three numbers played were quick ones and Molly's face took on a crazy wildness as he spun her round in a jive. Her body perspired and her head was dizzy but it did not matter, dancing was just brilliant. Then the music slowed down and the couples moved closer together.

David put his arms around Molly and held her close. She could smell the scent of his soap and it made her feel nervous in an excited sort of way. Then as he held her closer she could feel the heat of his body through his shirt. Even though she liked him very much she found it hard to relax in his arms. He was not familiar to her.

As they swayed and moved to the slow sensuous music, she was very aware that her breasts were pressing against his chest. Then just at that moment he smiled down at her.

What was he thinking? she wondered.

Then she felt his hardness against her leg and it was good to be in his arms. For the next two hours they jived and swayed to the music getting lost in the awareness of each other's body.

On the way home, as they chatted, they found that they both had a mutual love of rock and roll.

The van pulled up outside McDermotts and David switched off the engine. After successfully getting Luxemburg on the radio he leaned back in his seat and slid his arm slowly around Molly's shoulders. He caressed her hair as she sat nervously looking up at Jessie's bedroom window.

'I'll have to go in soon,' she said quietly.

'Are we going to have time for a kiss?' he asked taking her hand.

Molly smiled at him and he leaned over. As his face came nearer, she closed her eyes. His lips warm and gentle pressed tenderly down on hers but the kiss did not last very long.

Then David broke the silence by asking when he could see her again. Thinking for a minute she replied:

'I know,' she said eagerly, 'I could meet you tomorrow outside Hattie's. About two. I can leave my bike there.'

'Fair enough so,' he said as he started the engine.

Molly was a little disappointed that she did not get another kiss, but being polite she said nothing as she struggled with the door handle.

'Goodnight Molly.'

'Goodnight and thanks David,' she said as she turned and tiptoed into the quiet house.

CHAPTER TWENTY SEVEN

J.J. McDermott put his two elbows on the table, leaned over to Molly and said: ' There was an oul 'go the road' who used to call to the farm at home, and we were always amazed at how fast he could eat the dinner. But he wouldn't be in the halfpenny place with you me girl. 'What's the hurry?' asked Jessie curiously 'you'll only give yourself indigestion eatin' that fast.'

Suddenly Molly realized that they were both watching her and she slowed down.

'I'll go and get dessert now,' she said jumping up from the table.

'Aye do, and shur we might as well have the supper while your at it.'

J.J. winked at Jessie and they smiled. When she returned he asked more seriously;.

'Was it the dancing' last night that has you in such a hurry? or would you be goin' to meet your young man?'

'Well David said he'd call to see me today, but I told him I'd meet him at Hattie's.'

'Ah that explains it then,' said J.J. as he tucked into Jessie's tasty bread and butter pudding.

An hour later when Molly hopped up on the back of David's bike and put her arms around his waist she knew it all felt so right.

He weaved the machine effortlessly in and out of the traffic. The wind raced through Molly's long hair and her coat flew back revealing her long slender white legs. They sped past the large iron gates of the Phoenix Park and up and down the little hills and dips and hollows, eventually stopping beside a large oak tree.

'Oh David,' she said holding her hands up to her tingling cheeks,

'That was brilliant.'

'You liked it then?' he said as he got down.

'Oh yes, my bike seems so slow compared to this one.'

David sat down on the grass and watched her closely. She looked wonderful sitting up on his bike.

'Come over here and talk to me Molly,' he said as he patted the grass. Shyly she dismounted and walked towards him.

'I like it when you're near me,' he said, reaching out for her hand.'

'I like it too,' he said as she sat down easily and leaned back against the tree.

'Tell me about your farm in Wexford David, is it far away,?' she asked curiously.

'It's about sixty miles, but I can make it in two hours on the bike.'

'What animals are on it?'

'Horses, cattle, sheep, pigs, cats and dogs, and even rats. Everything really.'

'Ugh I don't like rats. Did you leave it because of the poverty ?'

'I don't know what you mean?' he said stroking her long silky hair.

'Well J.J. had to leave his farm because they were all hungry.'

Smiling at her innocence he replied: ' They were hard times then Molly but it is not like that today.'

'I don't really know much about farms,' she said awkwardly.

'Shur that's all right,' he said putting his arm reassuringly around her shoulder, ' I don't know much about fish.'

Then pulling her close to him he kissed her.

This time his kisses were slow and passionate and they awakened a new exciting feeling in Molly. Her lips melted into his. The wind rustled the leaves above as lying together under the tree, the evening sun warmed their bodies.

As she lay back in David's arms she listened intently as he told her all about his wonderful home in Wexford.

As the months passed Molly and David became inseparable. Their love for each other was evident in the light shining in their eyes. Their happiness spilled over to their families and friends. Everybody liked David very much indeed.

Although she spent every weekend with him Molly still kept Wednesday afternoons for Hattie. Their relationship grew as Molly began to confide in her about matters of the heart. The young romantic girl spent many hours listening to the older woman's advice about life and her courtship with her late husband James.

Seamus would often join the couple for a drink or a dance depending on his shift at the hospital. His fourth year of studies was a very busy one but he was enjoying his work immensely. More often than not he was accompanied by a pretty young nurse. She would laugh until her sides ached as he told her jokes and funny escapades about his time in Trinity. But for all his joking it seemed as if underneath he was searching for something and yet one had the feeling that he might never find it.

Molly and David did not see that much of William however as his life was so different from that of his brother. But they all kept in touch by long letters and remained very good friends.

While riding around Dublin City on the back of the bike, David pointed out many interesting buildings to Molly, and although she had walked by them many times, it was as if she was only really noticing them now. Like the Bank of Ireland, the only building in Europe with no windows. He taught her all about the different types of architecture and periods in which they were built. Molly came to be very proud of ones such as 'The Custom House' and 'Trinity College.' She loved the rows of Georgian houses all around St. Stephen's Green.

They explored the green parks together and spent many hours at the beautiful seasides in Bray and Donabate.

As they sped along the long coast road Molly held him tightly. Snuggling safely into his broad leather-clad back she felt like she was flying. Going to the theatre was extra special now, as they held hands all through the performance. It was at this time that the music heightened her sense of love and romance.

It was now five months since she had met David and they were the happiest of her life.

Then, one July evening as they were sitting in Stephen's Green park feeding the ducks, David asked her if she would like to come to Wexford. He had a week's holidays and he was going home. Molly did not have to be asked twice. She longed to see the Furlong farm he had often described.

'1 would love to meet your family and friends, especially Doireann.' she said excitedly.

David said nothing, his attention was suddenly drawn to a quarrel in the middle of the pond.

As he watched, he saw two little ducks desperately fighting over the one crust of bread.

CHAPTER TWENTY EIGHT

'It was a lovely summer's evening and Molly relaxed back into the passenger seat of David's new car.

'The car is lovely,' she said looking around at the leather interior of the red Volkswagen.

'I'm glad you like it,' he replied squeezing her hand.

'We should be in Wexford in two hours.'

Molly smiled back at him and they began exchanging all the news of the week. An hour later, with the city far behind them, she kicked off her shoes, wriggled her toes and relaxed.

The hills and valleys flashing by seemed endless. Flocks of sheep were dotted on the fields like woolly toys scrambling for higher grass. Houses in hollows were sheltered from harsh sea winds, while others stood out brazenly in defiance. Noticing this Molly wondered how people could ever build houses so high up on the hills.

'They probably carried it up stone by stone,' joked David.

'You're having me on now?' she said nudging his arm playfully.

How he loved teasing her.

'What are the people like in Wexford?'

'Salt of the earth really. Just ordinary country folk getting on with their lives. You need have no worries on that score Molly, they'll take to you alright.'

But she was worried. The countryside around her was so different from the Phoenix Park. This land was vast, rugged and wild. Suddenly she had a great urge to snuggle in closer to David. But for him being with her, she would have felt very lost.

Old ruins of castles and towers appeared from time to time on the landscape and she could almost visualise ghosts looking down from the battlements. David pointed out certain places of interest and she knew by the emotion in his voice that he really loved the land.

'Now Molly,' he said excitedly 'when we go round the next bend I want you to look down to your left, you should see the house.'

It was rather scary driving so high on the hillside but it was worth it for the view. She could see the chimney stacks standing among the tall trees.

The road dipped and turned for another half mile. Then suddenly from the top of the road she got her very first glimpse of Riversdale House.

The large house dominated the wooded valley but yet it looked extremely welcoming.

The long avenue up to it was bare with two enormous fields stretching out from either side.

Driving towards it the car was followed by a great cloud of white dust.

It was a big two-storey building, Georgian by design. Driving around into the back yard Molly was surprised to see a third storey.

Then stepping out of the car she was glad to be able to stretch her legs. The night air felt cool on her face and it was very refreshing.

Walter Furlong's imposing figure stood waiting in the doorway. David's father, a tall man with snow white hair and kind eyes.

'How ya son,' he said loudly as David removed the luggage from the boot.

'And who's this slip of a girl you've brought to see me?'

David put his arm around her and said smiling ,

'This is Molly, Molly Malone.'

After being welcomed heartily she stepped into a country kitchen. Smelling delicious home cooking she noticed a large old pine dresser standing against the back wall. The crockery displayed on it were shiny and colourful. The pine table was long and solid with matching chairs and although it was clean and warm the kitchen gave little evidence of a feminine touch.

Walter lifted the heavy kettle from the Aga cooker and poured the boiling water into a round teapot.

Molly noticed the tea tasted different from that at home. When she commented on its good flavour Walter proudly informed her it was the lime in the spring water that was responsible.

While David chatted to his father about his newcar Molly helped herself to some tasty looking buttered scones.

'1 have a few things to check on before I turn in,' said Walter rising from the table, 'David you show Molly her room and shur I'll see both of you in the morning.'

'Yes boss,' replied David.

Then smiling the old man tipped his scorched cap in her direction and went out into the farmyard.

Molly linked David up a wide staircase.

Outside the man in the moon looked in at her through the large lobby window.

Her room was small with a sloped ceiling, the curtains were drawn, and the bed covers turned down.' Em where's the bathroom please?' she whispered awkwardly.

Guiding her gently back out he pointed to a grey door at the end of the landing

When she returned a few moments later she found him sitting on her bed.

'Everything alright?' he enquired.

'Yes fine,' she answered as she sat down beside him.

'You won't get to meet Doireann and Frank until tomorrow. They usually go out on a Friday night.

He put his arms around her and held her close.

'You know you're the first girl I ever brought home and it feels good to have you here.'

'Your father's a lovely man,' she said shyly

Lifting her hair with his fingers he bent his head to kiss her neck.

'You know something Molly,' he whispered in between kisses.

'What's that? she said giggling and attractively tilting her head.

'He is lovely, and most people round here say I'm just like him.'

CHAPTER TWENTY NINE

Waking up to the sounds of the farm was very different from what Molly was used to. The cock crowing, geese babbling, dogs barking and buckets rattling.

Jumping out of bed she ran to the large window.

Pulling back the heavy curtains she found the different shades of green amazing. With her room situated at the front of the house she could see right across the fields. Two riders in the distance galloped by fast and furious. As they crossed the avenue, great clouds of white dust rose up at their feet. Approaching the long hedge on the far side, the first rider looked back at his companion. Molly gasped certain that he was unaware of how close the hedge was. Also frightened for his safety she immediately put her hands up to the window and went to call out. But then to her amazement the horse cleared the jump in one long stride

Rising effortlessly into the air the second rider did likewise. Then the two of them disappeared into the woods.

Molly began to dress quickly. Why didn't someone wake her up. She did not want to miss out on anything. Hurrying downstairs she looked around.

The clock on the wall said ten past eight, but it seemed nobody was about.

Out in the yard she could hear the tinkling of a bell and a strange buzzing sound. Following the noise she wandered into a building attached to the house. A young red-haired girl was separating milk with a strange machine.

'Excuse me,' shouted Molly '1 was looking for David.'

'Try the cowshed,' shouted the girl as without looking up she resumed her work.

But where was the cowshed? Molly did not know. Hurrying across the yard the geese flapped their wings and stretched their necks towards her. They also made a strange 'retching' sound. Opening a large wooden gate she entered a small courtyard. The sheds were redbrick and two stories high. It was almost like a little street but semicircular in design.

A wonderful old sun dial stood in the centre.

Walking into the nearest shed she saw cows all lined up in a row. Some kicked out at her as she passed but still she proceeded on nervously. At the end of it she thought she saw David's hands milking.

'Hello darling,' she said softly, but quickly blushed a bright red when she walked around the cow and saw Frank looking mischievously up at her instead.

His hair was like David's too but his features were rather boyish. 'Oh I thought you were David,' she said with embarrassment. 'Well I'm quare sorry I'm not,' he replied as they both simultaneously burst out laughing.

'I'm Molly,' she said stepping back a little.

'So your the girl Dave's talkin' to,' he said curiously.

Just then the loud clatter of horses hooves on the cobblestones echoed throughout the shed.

Molly looked out and was relieved to see David.

He was riding a beautiful black stallion and it excited her to see how confidently he handled it.

Behind him on a bay mare sat a young girl.

She wore cream jodhpurs and a black sloppy jumper. Removing her hat she shook out her thick wiry brown hair. Her skin was weathered and dark. She smiled down at Molly but her smile never reached her eyes. David jumped down from his horse and greeted her with a kiss.

'This is my sister Doireann,' he said affectionately.

'Nice dress.' the girl commented sarcastically.

The hot breath from David's horse was strong and forceful. Its black eyes stared wildly as he tossed his large head.

'Would it be Cuiteoig or me your afraid of ?' asked David noticing her nervousness.

'Well he is big,' replied Molly as she backed slowly away from the panting animal.

Doireann remained silent still seated on her horse.

She watched Molly closely.

David had said she was beautiful but it was her femininity that struck Doireann most. In her pretty dress and white sandals she looked as delicate as china.

Doireann knew that no matter how much she tried she could never look like that. Since her mother died when she was little she had been lost in a man's world.

Aggie Cullen had been no help.

The old housekeeper never ventured from the dark cross- over apron and the laced up boots.

As David and Molly exchanged glances it suddenly dawned on her how much David was smitten by this young Dublin girl.

After the two horses were stabled and fed David put his arm tenderly around Molly and guided her indoors for breakfast.

By the time Doireann entered the kitchen she could hear them laughing.

'What's so funny?' she asked.

'Molly thought young Biddy was you,' said David and he burst out laughing again.

'Did she now,' replied Doireann resentfully.

David spent the rest of the day bringing Molly on a guided tour of the large farm. He showed her all the places where they played as children.

Walking down a little laneway they came upon a miniature wood. The small trees were intertwined with eerie bare branches and the earth was soft and green beneath their feet. The Furlong children had nicknamed this wood 'Paradise', and had spent many long happy hours playing in it. It was their very own secret place and Aggie Cullen could never find them. Resting under the trees, David told Molly about his Mother's tragic death.

'The Boss was devastated and threw himself into the farm work. We were let run wild. Oh but Molly life was good then, and we didn't have a care. The summers were long and the winters magical.'

'Did Doireann miss her mother much?' asked Molly curiously.

'I suppose so, although she never said. She would tag along with Frank and me. Mind you she could run faster and jump higher than either of us. Yeah, she was a real little tomboy alright.' Later, that afternoon as they were strolling across the fields David pointed out a cottage in the distance. It's smoke was visible on the skyline.

'That's Aggie Cullen's cottage over there.'

'Can we go see her?' asked Molly excitedly.

'Maybe tomorrow, she never stirs out on a Sunday. We'll see.'

Molly found it very romantic strolling with David through the fields. Wild buttercups and daisies seemed like a carpet under their feet. He paused often and kissed her passionately under the clear blue skies. In Molly's heart she felt it really was a perfect day.

That evening everybody gathered in the kitchen for a cup of tea before making the seven mile journey. to a local dance in Courtown. Suddenly a very anxious Walter Furlong hurried in from the farmyard.

'I'm afraid you'll have to stay and help me Frank,' he said worriedly,' I'd say that cow will drop her calf this very night.'

Frank looked around disappointedly at everyone and began loosening his tie.

Sitting in the back of the car on the journey, Doireann remained quiet and thoughtful as she listened to David and Molly chatting. Although the ballroom was big and bright it was not as flashy as the building in Dublin, but the wonderful holiday atmosphere more than made up for that. While David twirled Molly around the floor she noticed Doireann talking to some men.

She liked the dress that Doireann had chosen to wear, but somehow she thought she had looked better in the trousers of the previous morning. Doireann in turn would steal glances at Molly. She watched her and David as they jived round the floor.

Then a roar went up from the crowd as the band announced the conga. A long line was soon formed. David grabbed the two girls and pushed them playfully in front of him. In the crush Molly found she was holding on to Doireann's waist. The older girl turned and smiled back at her, and for the first time since she arrived in Wexford Molly felt comfortable. They danced kicked and danced kicked, until the music stopped and everyone clapped.

Holding Molly close for the next slow number David was surprised when an old school-mate came over to them. His eyes looked glazed and staring with beads of sweat trickling down his shiny forehead. Leaning over he slapped his hot damp hand down on David's shoulder. Then in a drunken voice, and with a breath that smelled like a brewery he drawled:

'Hey Dave, I wouldn't mind gettin' her under the Skeogh tree tonight.' Shrugging the hand off his shoulder David held Molly even tighter to him.

'Well now Dick,' he replied as he moved away,' that would make a change, your usually there on your own.'

The man took another sip of frothy Guinness from a messy pint glass that was held shakily in his hand, and slowly turned away.

It had been a marvellous night's dancing, and they talked about everyone who had been there on the way home, Doireann stayed up late and recalled the whole event to Frank when he came into the kitchen. Tired from dancing, David and Molly excused themselves and went up totheir rooms.

The calf had been delivered safely and Frank was enjoying a well earned cup of tea.

'Do ya think is David serious about her,' asked Doireann, toying with her teaspoon.

'I think so,' replied Frank as he rinsed out his mug. 'And there's a thing Doireann,' he continued 'if they get married, the chances are they could come back here to live.'

Frank's words were very worrying.

A real fear gripped Doireann's heart as she realized that the day might just come soon when she'd have to leave Riversdale House.

CHAPTER THIRTY

After Mass the next day, Biddy proudly served up a mouth-watering Sunday lunch. Since Molly had come to Wexford she found the country air had given her an enormous appetite. Mashed potatoes, roast beef, garden peas and carrots were all enhanced by a wonderful thick gravy.

For dessert, the fresh cream from the dairy went very well with the cool strawberry jelly.

'Mr. Furlong, what was Hattie like growing up.' asked Molly curiously. Walter thought carefully for a moment.

'Hard workin' enough, spent most of her time with her head stuck in a book. That's probably where she got all her fancy ideas from. Always dressing up dolls she was, and even the cat if it sat still long enough. Her and James came down to visit us a lot in the first year of their marriage. I remember when poor Doris died, God rest her, she wanted to bring Doireann to Dublin to live with them. But I hadn't the heart to let the child go. Strange, we were never as close afterwards.'

Then looking over at Doireann he smiled,

'Mind you there's times when I'm quare sorry I didn't let ya go.'

Everyone knew by Doireann's expression that she didn't find his remarks one bit funny.

After lunch David and Molly strolled over in the direction of Aggie's house.

When David opened the garden gate they found a white-haired old woman sitting on a wooden plank. Some cats lay sleeping around her feet.

Surprised to see people coming through the gate she quickly removed a white dugeen from her mouth, quenched the tobacco with her thumb and slid it quickly into her pocket.

Then noticing David coming up behind Molly she stood up and greeted him saying:

'Ah Master David, is it yourself,' she said looking up at him.

'Yes Aggie, it's me, how are you?' 'Sur I'm fine, and who's this you've brung to see me? Would it be the girl yer courtin' by any chance?'

'Yes Aggie, I'd like you to meet Molly Malone.'

Molly held out her soft white hand and Aggie's dark wrinkled ones encircled it warmly.

'Ya'll come and sit with me awhile will ya?' she asked as she turned and walked slowly into the cottage.

The kitchen was dark with a funny smokey smell. Over a large open fireplace hung a picture of the sacred heart.

All around on ledges chipped mugs and pots held half burned out candles. An old settle-bed in the corner looked cosy and there were a lot of old coats hanging beside the chimney breast.

Aggie wiped a stool for Molly to sit down and was about to remove some old coats when David told her not to fuss. He preferred to sit on the forum, his usual spot.

'You're not a country person are ya,' the old woman asked Molly

'No I'm from Dublin,' replied Molly shyly.

'Hah I knew that. Ya always had an eye for the pretty ones Master David.' she said as she broke out into a hoarse laugh.

'I'll wet the tay now, and I've a griddle cake just done in the pan.' Molly was about to refuse as she was full after the wonderful lunch in Furlong's, but David motioned to her to say nothing. While Aggie informed David of all the local goings on, Molly looked around the kitchen and she noticed a little table over in the corner.

The linen covering it was discoloured. Two candles in silver holders stood each side of a framed photograph. A handsome soldier smiled out from behind the brown glass. Lying under the picture the chain of a small locket was intertwined with a gold wedding ring.

Molly wondered about it but could not bring herself to ask. At the fireplace a black iron kettle hung from the crane over the fire. Using a long tongs Aggie removed the baker and leaning in she lifted out a large griddle cake with the corner of her apron.

The tea was strong and dark and when she poured the milk in, dollops of cream floated on top. Aggie broke the cake in half and cut it into long thin slices.

The yellow butter melted slowly into it. Molly was surprised at how good it tasted.

'Any word of Hattie's boys?' Aggie asked caringly.

'Seamus is almost a doctor now and next year William will be ordained. They're both very well.' replied Molly.

'Glory be to God a priest in the family. That's a blessin' ya know,' and she made the sign of the

cross on her chest. Then she enquired "What are ya me girl.'

'I work for my Uncle in a fish shop.'

'And would ya rise early.'

'About half seven, the shop is open from eight till six.'

'So your not afraid of hard work then?'

'No,' laughed Molly.

'Are your parents livin'?'

'My mother died having me and I never knew my father, he went off to sea.'

Aggie went quiet for a moment. She glanced over at the photograph and then gazed thoughtfully into the fire.

'There's a lot of menfolk lost in that sea,' she said sadly.

'A lotta lost souls walkin' under and over that cold water. Then again there's a lotta good people waitin' for them to come home. Yer mother's dead ya say? Died when ya were young ya say? Well Master David, I believe that mothers taken from their young always come back to guide their ways.

Then turning towards David she said mysteriously,

'I'm glad you brought her here.'

On hearing these words David looked over at Molly. He wondered if it could be her mothers presence that she had always felt in the wind. Then he too wondered if his own mother was watching over him. Looking at his watch he winked at Molly and stood up.

'We must be off now Aggie,' he said, rising from his seat, 'But we'll come again before we leave on Friday.'

Then slipping her a ten shilling note he added caringly:

'There's something for yourself.'

Aggie looked down at the money and thanked and blessed him.

'Wait now,' she said grabbing Molly's arm as they went to go. 'I have something for ya lass.'

Then she went over to a small dresser and pulled out a drawer. It seemed to the two young people she might never find what she was looking for. But they stood patiently waiting as they smiled at one another.

Eventually after much rummaging she found it.

Walking slowly back to Molly she held out her hand and in the centre lay a beautiful silver miraculous medal and chain.

'Wear this always and no harm will come to ya. It belonged to the mistress herself, God be good to her. She would want David's love to have it.'

David helped fasten the medal around Molly's neck and she bent and gave the old woman an affectionate kiss.

Looking a bit flustered Aggie muttered : 'Off with ya now child and shur I'll see ya again, please God.'

As they walked down the little path she watched them until they were out of sight.

Turning she bent down and picked up a small black cat.

Cradling and stroking it in her arms she walked back into her lonely kitchen.

Wandering over to the little table she picked up the soldiers picture.

A large tear rolled down her wrinkled old face and she brushed it away with the back of her hand.

'It's their time now Tommy darlin', she said softly

'It's their time now.'

CHAPTER THIRTY ONE

After the quiet relaxing mood of Sunday, Monday morning brought a flurry of excitement to the farmyard.

When Molly arrived down for breakfast Biddy had the hard boiled eggs already on the table. Molly looked over at the window and noticed that there were some strange men standing in groups outside in the yard. When she enquired as to who they were Biddy replied smartly:

'They be the journey men miss.'

'What do ya mean journey men?' asked Molly curiously.

'They're men that come from anywhere and everywhere. They go from farm to farm helpin' with the hay makin'.'

'That's nice of them,' said Molly.

Biddy rolled around the kitchen laughing.

'What's so funny?' asked Molly.

'Shur they have to be fed and paid ya know,' she said smugly.

Outside in the yard David stood beside the men as he yoked up a big carthorse. As soon as Molly had finished her breakfast she went out to join him.

Reaching up to the large quiet animal she stroked him and in turn, he nibbled her hand with his big velvety lips.

'He's called Boley,' said David 'We've had him for years.'

A little way off, Walter was handing out pitchforks to the journey men. They took turns to stare at Molly while she noticed they had some twine tied under the knees of their trousers.

Then Frank drove a grey tractor into the yard with a buck rake mounted behind.

Some of the men jumped up on the rake to go down the fields.

'I'm afraid we'll be at the hay all day Molly,' said David seriously

'Doireann's gone into town to get more twine and some groceries. Would you mind if I asked you to give Biddy a hand with the dinner.?'

'Of course I wouldn't mind,' replied Molly eagerly

'I'll be glad to have something to do.'

Giving her arm an affectionate squeeze, David went over and joined the Boss.

Then they turned and left the yard. The long chains rattled on either side of Boley as they followed the tractor.

The hot sun was climbing high in the sky and all the signs pointed to it being a very warm day.

When everyone was gone, a lonely silence descended on the old place and Molly returned to the kitchen to help Biddy, just as she was arriving in from the garden carrying four large cabbages.

Struggling to lift them onto the draining board she said worriedly;

'I've a lot to do today Miss, the Boss says there's twelve for dinner.'

'I'll help if you like,' offered Molly 'but you'll have to show me what to do.'

Biddy smiled to herself as she liked being in charge, .

'I'll wash the spuds and you Miss could chop the cabbage, you'll get a big knife over in that drawer.'

The two girls chatted while they worked and Molly told Biddy all about her life in Dublin.

They were so engrossed in their conversation that they did not hear Doireann return.

Walking in the door carrying a large box of groceries she was annoyed to see Molly working in her kitchen, but she took her anger out on poor Biddy.

'I thought I told you we'd start dinner when I got back,' she snapped.

'Sorry Mam, but Master David said...'.

'Since when did he start gettin' the dinner round here?' she said crossly, plonking the groceries on the table.

Trying to ease the situation Molly offered to help Doireann.

'No thanks I can manage; Biddy would ya go and wash up the dairy.'

With her offer of help refused Molly decided to go back upstairs to her room. The house was lonely without David. She wandered over to the window and looked out across the avenue.

Hugging her arms she wondered how far away the hayfield was.

Sitting alone in her room, her thoughts turned towards Roseanne. So she decided to write a long letter to her friend.

It was two years since Roseanne's baby was adopted and she had found a good job in an Irish pub in London.

From the last letter Molly had received, it seemed like Roseanne and the manager had a little romance going.

Some time later with the letter finished and the sealed envelope sitting on the dressing table she returned to the kitchen. Biddy and Doireann were busy outside packing large pots into the back of a Morris Oxford.

Walking out to join them Doireann ignored her completely. Then as she was getting into the car she looked her up and down indignantly. Still disapproving of her flimsy city clothes she said in a matter of fact way. 'I suppose you better come to the hayfield with us.'

Molly was delighted for she could not wait to see David again. The ride was very bumpy across two large fields but it was worth it. The hot sun reflecting on the haystacks turned the whole field into gold. Here and there wisps of hay sparkled in the brilliant light. Through the haze of sunshine she strained her eyes to catch sight of David.

Eventually, they came to a shaky stop and Doireann blew the horn.

The journey men looked up from their hard work, downed tools and made their way towards the car. The girls jumped out and began unloading the food. Hot spuds were piled high in a large black pot while the cabbage was in a smaller one. Bacon cut up in slices were wrapped in cloth and the salt was in a little sack. Molly lifted out the heavy churn and struggled with the lid. One of the men came to her assistance saying;

'Here Lass the daylight's passin','

Molly stood back and watched his big strong hand effortlessly twist open the lid. Then after each man dipped his mug in, he knelt down on one knee and ate hungrily from the heaped plate on the ground.

Boley walked slowly across the field with David sitting up behind and Molly hurried over to meet them. When he pulled a lever the teeth of the rake rose up and he fastened it with a clip. Then jumping down from his seat, he coiled the reins and hung them loosely on the hames. Sitting with David while he ate his dinner Molly wondered why there were small cocks of hay placed around the ditch.

'There hobblers,' he said as he enjoyed his lunch ' and there a bit wet today so we'll put them in cocks tomorrow.'

'Is Frank making hobblers with the tractor?' she enquired as she sucked on a traithnin..

'No he's actually plotting it for the men to put in cocks.'

It all seemed very complicated to her and a lot of hard work. When they had all eaten their fill the journey men sat chatting for a while. Walter called his two sons over to give them instructions for the rest of the afternoon. He pointed this way and that and while he was speaking Molly studied the three of them.

They were big Wexford men with a quiet strength. Standing together in the middle of the field they looked like they could face almost anything. Her attention was suddenly drawn to Walter's wispy white hair as it lifted gently with the summer breeze. Then a sadness came over her as she thought and wondered about her own father. Then Walter Furlong turned around and gave an order and the journey men jumped up quickly.

The girls reloaded the car and everyone got back to work.

As Molly lifted the churn Doireann shouted across at her.

'Leave that for the men, and make sure the lid's on tight or the hayseeds will blow in.'

Molly put the churn back down on the ground and was about to get into the car when David came up behind her. Catching her arm he whispered in her ear,

'Why don't you stay for a while?'

She was happy to stay and rather relieved. The atmosphere back at the house was a little strained and so, for the next three hours she decided to explore the hay field.

With outstretched arms she playfully ran up and down the windrows. Then turning, she would repeatedly go back and jump over them again. She had never felt such freedom before. It was exhilarat-ing. Breathlessly, she lay back against one of the haycocks. A gentle wind rose up to cool her face and she instinctively knew she was not alone.

After some time she heard the sound of the cuckoo in the distance. Wondering if she could see it she got up quickly and followed the sound.

It led her across the field and over to the headlands. Curiously she paced up and down the hedgerows straining her ears. She was sure the bird was in the next field. She began searching for an opening in the hedge and, finding one, she pushed her way carefully through the briars and weeds.

Then to her amazement she saw a field like green velvet stretching out before her. The bird was instantly forgotten. In wonder she stood and watched the sun playfully chase the shadows across the slopes. It seemed to Molly that the hand of God was stroking the corn and that the leafy blades were bowing humbly to His divine touch.

As she stood and marvelled at the beauty of it all a mysterious fear came over her and she suddenly wanted to be back in the safety of the hayfield and be with David.

Turning, she ran through the hedge, forgetting to be careful this time. The thorns pricked her legs as she hurried on. She had just reached David when Doireann's car turned into the hayfield.

'Oh good, your back,' he said smiling, 'I was wondering where you got to. Here's Doireann with the four o'clock tea.'

Deciding to tell him all about the cornfield later she helped Doireann hand round the hot tea and the big meaty sandwiches.

This time, with everything packed in the car she returned to the house.

In an awkward silence the three girls prepared their evening meal, and after a hard day's work everyone retired to bed early.

The haymaking continued with an urgency all the next day and Molly saw little of David. Spending more time with Biddy she tried to keep out of Doireann's way. Following Biddy around the farm she learned how to feed hens, collect eggs, separate milk and make butter. But watching how she milked the cows was best of all.

First she washed the cows udder with warm water and a cloth. Then taking the teat in one hand she squirted some milk into the other cupped one. Then dipping her fingers in her palm she rubbed the milk on to the cows teats. Taking hold of the back teats first she began milking the cow.

The warm milk squirted with a 'whi who' into the big metal bucket. When she was finished she dipped her thumb into the warm suds and made the sign of the cross on the cow's hip.

By six o'clock that evening the haymaking was all over. The journey men handed back their pitchforks and loosened the twine on their trousers. Walter paid each man for his work and they thanked him gratefully. Then, tipping their Caps respectfully, they turned and left the yard.

However, one big burly character took the money eagerly, held it in his hand and then spat on it.

'I'll be back for the harvest Mr. Furlong sir,' he grinned 'and the balance of the day to ya all.'

CHAPTER THIRTY TWO

Molly searched through the woods and hedgerows. The sound of the cuckoo grew louder. She looked this way and that, searching. Then suddenly she saw it, sitting on the scales of the shop counter. Stretching out her arm she opened her hand gently, and was about to grasp it when a voice sounded in her ear:

'Wake up Darling, wake up.'

Suddenly the bird disappeared.

'What time is it?' she asked with heavy tired eyes shut tightly.

'It's seven o'clock,' replied David kissing her cheek.

But the bird... It was so real... but she must have been dreaming.

'Would you like to come to the fair with us?' he whispered.

'Oh yes but what will I wear.'

'A jumper and trousers will do. Its a bit cooler today. Now hurry down for breakfast, Frank and the Boss are ready to go.'

As soon as he left the room she jumped out of bed.

'Why don't they ever call me in time,' she thought as she dressed hurriedly. Then after grabbing a quick cup of tea, she hurried outside and climbed into the back seat of the car.

It was ten miles as the crow flies to the fair in Carnew.

The Furlong men were off to buy a cow.

Occasionally they were stopped by drovers flagging them down. Herds of cattle walked nervously past the car, sometimes it seemed too close for comfort. Molly held David's hand tightly.

'We'd want to be careful now we don't buy a kicker,' said Walter watching them pass, 'a nice polly shorthorn is what we want.'

His sons readily agreed with him.

It seemed like everyone in Wexford was heading towards the fair. Men, women and children hurried along the road, all carrying something.

Stalks of rhubarb, hawks of onions, cabbage plants and parsnips. Peculiar shaped sacks were slung over handlebars of bikes and it was anyone's guess as to what was in them.

Eventually they arrived and Frank parked the car under the shade of the trees. David opened the door and helped Molly out.

Her idea of a fair was stalls of fruit and vegetables, maybe some clothes and jewellery. But she was unprepared for the sight that met her eyes. People shouting, children running wildly around chasing frightened animals, asses braying, dogs barking and cows and calves mooing.

It was very noisy and there seemed to be no order to anything. Then in the middle of all the primitive chaos she suddenly noticed the smell. It was like farmyard manure only stronger. Her face flinched as she tried to hold her breath. Taking her hand David walked in front of her as he made his way through the crowd. Annoyingly flies were everywhere. She kept her eyes mostly on the ground trying hard to avoid stepping into the cow droppings. Every so often David would stop to chat to a friend or neighbour and she would shuffle from foot to foot impatiently, hoping that he would soon move on.

There were a lot of animals to view at the fair and by lunch time they had all worked up quite an appetite.

Walter suggested a meal in the 'eatin house' close by and once inside Molly excused herself and made straight for the toilets, but it was not a pretty sight.

With the seat broken and the floor wet she decided maybe it would be better to hang on for a bit.

On returning to the restaurant she found that the food on the table was off-putting too as the smell from the toilets wafted in the air. The men however did not seem to notice at all but Molly just could not finish her meal.

After lunch they began looking at the cows in earnest. There were at least thirty or forty to be examined if they were to buy the right one.

David and Frank stooped to check the udders.

If the cow kicked while being examined it meant she would do the same during milking. Some of the cows had very full udders indeed and the milk from them was trickling down onto the ground. Dirty stray dogs running around licked it up thirstily. Molly was not comfortable at all being at the fair and she wished the Furlong men would hurry up. Surely it could not take this long to buy a cow.

Then, in the midst of all the squalor she looked around and saw a well dressed woman walking towards them.

She was about Hattie's age but smaller in height. She wore a brown fleece-lined jacket with a long tweed skirt. Her greying hair was almost concealed beneath a very flashy hat, and except for some red lipstick, her small tanned face was devoid of any makeup.

But her smile was genuine and her handshake warm.

'Well David', she said smiling 'I heard you were home.'

'That's right Lady Gowne just for the week.'

'And who is this delightful young woman may I ask?' she said looking curiously at Molly.

'This is Molly Malone.'

'Well how do you do?' she said and offered to shake her hand.

'Hello,' replied Molly shyly as she in turn took it.

'I was hoping you both would join me for some tea. The Hotel's quite near and you can always look at those cows later.'

To Molly's ears it was the best suggestion all day. She tugged discreetly at David's sleeve.

'Okay we've finished here anyway,' he said

'It's up to the Boss now to make his choice.

'Once inside the hotel Molly excused herself and made for the ladies. This time she found it clean and presentable.

'I must say David she is a very pretty girl.' observed Lady Gowne as she removed her jacket.

'Yes I think so too.' he replied as he pulled out a chair for her.

'Thank you, now tell me, she said,

'Is there 'anything doin' as they say.'

With a mischievous look on his face David replied:

'Could well be my lady, could very well be.'

'Well I'm glad, it's high time you settled down.

Why I was well married with two children by the time I was thirty.'

Just then Molly rejoined them as the waitress was pouring the tea. The moist chocolate cake looked delicious.

Then the conversation turned towards horses.

'Tell me David,' she said, winking at Molly,

'Are we going to have a deal over that wonderful black hunter of yours?'

'I'm afraid Cuiteoig is not a lady's ride.'

'Come now, you know I was riding before you were born.'

'Oh that may well be Lady Gowne,' said David respectfully, 'but personally I don't believe anyone else could handle him. He is very hot-blooded and stands seventeen hands high.

Quite frankly you would be over-horsed.'

'1 see,' she said thoughtfully as she passed the sugar around.

'Well then, I've another idea, when my mares come in use next spring perhaps you would let him cover some of them.?'

'We'll see,' he replied as he watched Molly refilling the tea cups. 'If he winters well and looks good after the hunting season I'll consider it then.'

'I'll make it worth your while,' she said earnestly,' but it would be a strictly no foal no fee basis.'

'God you're a tough woman Lady Gowne,' he laughed.

'One has to be in this business eh Molly?' she said smiling over at the young girl. 'Anyway, perhaps in the near future one of my mares might throw a colt just like him and then we'd both have what we want eh?'

Then turning to Molly she continued;

'You must get David to bring you over to visit me sometime. I will show you all my horses and the plans for my new indoor stables.'

'I'd like that.' replied Molly as she helped herself to another slice of cake.

They spent the next hour chatting and would still be there but for Frank interrupting them.

Hurrying in the door he greeted Lady Gowne and told David that the Boss was ready to leave.

They all rose from the table and walked together to the main entrance of the hotel. As she was leaving, Lady Gowne once more extended her invitation to Molly to visit her at her home near Mount Benedict.

Walking across the square David enquired from Frank as to which cow his father had bought.

'The nice polly shorthorn. Ya know the one belongin' to the man with the big elder from Bunclody,' replied Frank happily.

A little way off they saw Walter standing chatting to a man with a horse and creel. The creel was full of bonhams and as they drew nearer they realized that he had bought one.

Frank climbed into the creel and amidst much sorting on his behalf, and screeching on the pigs, he picked out the biggest one.

Walter stood patiently holding the sack. Frank carefully dropped the shrieking pig into it, then after tying the top of the sack with a piece of twine he put it in the boot of the car.

'Will it not suffocate in there?' asked Molly worriedly.

Walter laughed on hearing this and taking the sack out again he said:

'Not the slightest fear of it, now that's what a pig in a poke is.'

On the journey home Molly pondered on all the strange words she had heard that day; It was like a different language. There was an awful lot more to learn about the countryside then she . ever realized. It had a hidden culture all of its own.

Noticing how quiet she had become David put his arm around her and asked considerately:

'Well did you enjoy the fair darling?'

'Yes…in a way.' she replied smiling.

'Would you come with me again?'

Nestling very comfortably in his arms she replied: ' Maybe in my dreams.'

CHAPTER THIRTY THREE

It was her last day in Wexford and Molly woke early. Putting on her dressing gown she walked over and sat at the window of her bedroom. She never tired of watching David and Doireann ride across the fields and she had to admit to herself that Doireann was a great horsewoman.

Sitting astride her white horse she had such great confidence and control.

Feeling little pangs of jealousy, she knew horse riding was the one thing she could never share with David.

She liked horses but she was afraid of them too.

After listening to the conversation yesterday between Lady Gowne and David, she realized that unless she learned to ride she would miss out on a lot of the excitement of the countryside.

When the David and Doireann returned to the yard Molly was waiting for them. She walked over to David and asked him to teach her to ride.

After thinking for a few moments he told her that the only one suitable was Doireann's horse Pacha.

'I think Boley would suit her better,' replied Doireann quickly.

Ignoring her sarcastic comment David suggested that Lady Gowne might have a quiet horse.

'The next time we come down I'll ask her about it, it's too late now Molly, we're going back to Dublin early in the morning.'

Walking with him towards the house, Molly wanted to tell him about Doireann's mean attitude towards her. But then she thought she might sound a little childish. Anyway, the next time they returned to Wexford, she just might become more friendly.

'It will be a while before I get to ride Cuiteoig again Molly,' would you mind if I went out again this afternoon?'

'No of course not,' she said smiling, 'I'll go for a walk around the place and I'll see you when you get back.'

After lunch she watched David ride out on Cuiteoig. The horse's black coat shone like velvet and his tail waved high in the air behind him. He was a powerful swift animal, and David and him were like one as they cantered out the gate and across the fields.

After meeting so many people all week Molly found it quite nice to be alone for a while and she decided to stroll off in the direction of 'Paradise '.

From an upstairs bedroom window Doireann watched her go. The events of the past week went over in her mind and she remembered especially how David always looked lovingly at Molly.

Slowly a heavy grinding ache began to gnaw at her insides. Only once had she, Doireann, known such love and attraction. But the boy she had fallen for had been snatched from her by another girl with hair like Molly's. Turning from the window she caught sight of her reflection in the dressing table mirror. Fingering her tousledcoarse hair, she sighed as she said enviously:

'Oh why don't I have lovely hair like that, or eyes so wonderfully blue?'

Then taking a closer look into the mirror her gaze wandered over her face. She hated how she looked. She felt ugly, fat and masculine. She knew she was more comfortable on a horse than in a dress. Not bearing to look at herself any more she turned once more from the mirror, and went back to the window.

Below her she saw Molly stop to talk to Walter and Frank. The three of them burst out laughing. Molly had won Frank over but then she would.

When it came to women Frank was easily led.

He always fell for the obvious.

With the Boss however it was different. He had told Doireann that Molly reminded him of his late wife, her mother, so feminine and gentle. Suddenly the sound of their laughter filled the bedroom. Doireann began to think that they were laughing at her. Feeling very alone, a sudden anger boiled up inside her as more silly jealous thoughts came into her mind.

Looking down at Molly she felt she hated her. She hated her having David's love, she hated her beauty and her smile, but most of all she hated the fact that one day she might be Mistress of Riversdale House. In that moment she knew she would have to have it out with her.

Turning quickly from the window she picked the riding crop from the dressing table and hurried from the room.

Out in the front yard Molly was unaware of the hatred that was looking down on her. She said goodbye to the men and continued walking towards the wood. She was so happy. She need not have feared coming to Wexford at all. She had fitted in so well. She really felt at home in Riversdale House.

As she walked slowly through the field her spirit was at ease. The sun warmed her body and gentle breeze played with her light summer dress. The grass tickled her toes through her sandals and it felt cool to the touch.

Looking up at the clear blue sky she had a sudden urge to speak to her mother:

'1 love him Mammy,' she said almost prayerlike.

'I love him so much. Thank you God for sending him to me.'

Just then the hooves of a horse was heard in the distance and, thinking it was David, she turned, only to see Doireann coming towards her.

Galloping like hell's fire across the wide field Doireann's whip came down hard and fast on Pacha..

The speed of the horse and the cool breeze on her face only served to heighten her blind temper. As she approached Molly she brought the horse to a sudden halt by pulling hard on the reins.

'So here you are Madam,' she shouted at her.

Molly was shocked, and the shock caused her to stand very still.

'What's wrong Doireann?' she managed to utter.

'I'll tell you what's wrong you little nobody. You think you can come down here to my house and my farm with my brother and take over. You with your ridiculous clothes and your stupid smile.'

'But Doireann I didn't,' said Molly trying to move back from the panting horse.

'This is my land you hear, and this is my place,' she screamed, 'I won't let you take it from me.'

Doireann's face had become twisted with anger and for a moment Molly did not recognize her.

Frightened, she turned to run away but her foot twisted in her sandal and she fell on the grass.

Still in her mad temper Doireann raised her leather whip as if to strike Molly. Suddenly a great storm rose up and forcefully encircled both horse and rider.

While raising her arm to protect her eyes, Doireann dropped the whip.

Sensing the supernatural, the horse whinnied and reared its front legs. Molly was sure he was going to kick her. In sheer terror she bowed her head and started to cry. Doireann wrestled hard with the reins trying to bring Pacha under control but the wind howled and tore at her clothes with such violence that she eventually lost her grip and fell painfully down on the hard ground. Immediately Pacha broke free and galloped across the fields towards the headlands and David. Noticing the horse with no rider David galloped Cuiteoig in the direction it had come from. Fearing an accident he was relieved to see the girls moving in the distance. Riding over to them he dismounted quickly. The wind had subsided and everything calmed down. He did not know which of them to go to first. Molly sat sobbing and crying and Doireann sat motionless as if she had seen a ghost.

'What on earth happened here,?' he asked worriedly.' I've just seen Pacha tear across the field as if the devil himself was after him.'

Molly stood up and ran crying towards the wood.

Kneeling down on one knee he took Doireann by the shoulders, 'You better tell me now what happened here,' he said angrily.

In a rather shaky voice she told him about the argument and how the wind rose up and knocked her off the horse.

'What were you arguing about?'

'I just told her that she would never be mistress here. This is my place, this is my land.'

Running his hand frustratingly through his black fringe, his eyes grew angry and he said:

'How dare you treat my girlfriend like that. She would never have even thought of it. Why she is not like you or I. She moves through this world and yet seems not to be part of it. She doesn't hanker after possessions or places, it is her spirit that make her happy. I don't know where you would get that terrible idea from.'

Looking a little shame faced down at the ground Doireann said quietly, 'I got it from Frank.'

'Frank,' he shouted. 'and what would he know about anything. He doesn't care about God, man or the devil, and he never goes to church mass or meeting. I don't give a tuppeny damn about Frank, but I do care about Molly.'

Then looking across the fields towards the house he continued:

'I'm telling you now Doireann, Molly will be my wife but not here. We will find our own place. Your precious house and lands are safe.

But in years to come when your strolling around them on your own, you remember today and what you've done. I only hope you can forgive yourself.'

She watched him as he mounted Cuiteoig and galloped off to find Molly. He caught up with her at the entrance to the wood. She was sobbing bitterly as if her heart would break. He jumped down off his horse and tied the reins to the nearest tree. Then taking her hand he led her towards the wood. Whenever he had any special thing in childhood he would bring it here to paradise.

Now he felt he was in danger of losing the most precious thing in his whole life.

Under the shade of the trees he stood with his back to the rough bark. Molly put her arms around his waist and cried bitterly into his chest. Her tears wet his shirt and, even though he knew she was upset, her closeness excited him. He bent his head and kissed her eyes.

In response to his tenderness a spontaneous passion rose up between them. Slowly she raised her eyes and looked up at him. His arms encircled her neck and he pulled her closer. Their light summer clothes were no barrier against their desires.

Her breasts swelled and her hips swayed as his hands caressed her body.

'I love you Molly and I want you.' He moaned.

'1 love you too David,' she whispered and their kisses built up to a hunger yearning to be satisfied. He gently lowered her down on the soft mossy earth, the heat of his hand arousing her further.

As he explored her body his lips searched longingly for her soft round breasts.

Never had she felt such excitement run through her warm veins. He had awakened her passion of uncontrollable desire.

Molly's blood was on fire.

He pressed his hard body down on hers and her soft body arched up to meet him.

Her legs relaxed and in that instant an unwelcome frightening thought entered her mind. Roseanne.

This was what must have happened to Roseanne.

God now she knew. Oh no, what if it were to happen right here, right now with David. Then a real fear gripped her heart and she remembered Tom O' running out. Suddenly David's passion became threatening to her and she began to push him away. Unaware of her thoughts David kept on kissing and caressing her. Again she pushed harder and this time she managed to break free. Sitting up she pulled her dress down and protectively hugged her knees

'What is it Molly?' he asked worriedly

'I'm afraid,' she said and started crying again.

Putting his arms around her he asked gently,

'Did I hurt you?'

'No,' she said tearfully.

'Well what is it then? Tell me please.'

Turning to look at him she said very seriously:

'I'm afraid that if I get pregnant you'll leave me.'

Taking her hands he gently pulled her up to a standing position, holding her close he looked up at the sky, then stroking her lovely silky hair he whispered tenderly,

'Oh Molly...Oh Molly.'

Then taking her face gently in his hands he said in a very tender voice:

'Don't cry darling, today I have realized something for the first time since I met you. If you were to leave me I would die. Finding you is like finding the other half of my soul. Your beauty is wonderful, but darling it is nothing compared to what I see in your eyes. When you look at me I see love that is deep and true. When I hold you I know I hold a love that is mine, and when I kiss you I feel like...I'm in Heaven. Marry me, Molly, let me be yours forever.'

His loving words broke through all her unwanted fears.

Her heart suddenly soared and smiling up at him she replied positively:

'Oh yes David I will marry you.'

They embraced and once more kissed passionately.

As she relaxed in his arms a poem he had learned in his childhood suddenly came back to him and he whispered it into her ear.

'If I could catch and hold this time,
I know that I would find,
A heaven on this earth below,
a treasure that would bind.
Our hearts as one, our souls entwined,.
Our minds and bodies free,
and you and I together love,
forever we would be.'

CHAPTER THIRTY FOUR

On Friday morning Walter Furlong walked into the kitchen in the same quiet way he had done for years. With his braces over his shirt he sat down on his chair at the end of the table. His place was already set with breakfast dishes from the night before, and as he turned his cup upwards on the saucer he noticed an uneasy silence among his children.

'What's up?' he asked, 'Did someone die and your not tellin' me.'

'No,' said David angrily, 'But someone could have been killed yesterday afternoon.'

'How's that,' replied Walter curiously.

Looking accusingly across the kitchen at Doireann and Frank David continued:

'Because of one careless remark from Frank, Doireann took it in her head that Molly was going to come here and take over.'

'Is this true Doireann?' he asked quietly.

'Well, yeah,' she said hesitantly, 'I thought because David was the eldest that if they got married, they would live here.'

'And what had you to do with this Frank?"

'I just said it, I didn't mean nothin'.'

'You said what?' asked Walter, his tone becoming a little louder. David interrupted.

'I'll tell you what he said Boss, and I'll tell you what she did,' he said pointing at Doireann.

'She chased after Molly with her horse and nearly ran her down, that's what she did.'

'Good God,' said Walter worriedly,' Is the child alright? where is she now?'

'She's okay, she's upstairs packing, no thanks to them.'

'But Daddy,' protested Doireann, 'This wind came out of nowhere and frightened Pacha. It threw me to the ground. That one is some kind of witch.'

'Now don't go makin' excuses Doireann, what I want to know is, did you try and harm that little girl?'

'Well no I just got angry.'

Walters eyes darkened and he rose slowly from his chair.

Placing his hands on either side of the table he looked from one to the other.

'Listen you three, both me and your mother has put blood, sweat and tears into rearin' yeze, yeze mightened have always had what you wanted, but we always made damn sure yeze had what you needed. Lord, your mother would turn in her grave if she thought yeze grew up so ungrateful. To think yeze would start fighten' among yourselves as to who's goin' to get the place before I even close me eyes.'

Then his hand came down with a heavy thud on the table.

'I will say this once. This farm is mine and it will be my decision as to who will live here after me. But I'm tellin' ya now I'll burn the house to the ground and sell the land rather than let yeze fight over it.'

Then too upset to eat his breakfast he took his cap from the cooker rail and walked out the door.

Frank and Doireann were too ashamed to raise their embarrassed eyes from the floor.

At eleven, Molly and David were all packed and ready for their journey back to Dublin.

Walter took her hand firmly in his and pulled her close with the other one.

'You're welcome in my home as long as I live,' he said affectionately.

'Thanks Mr. Furlong,' she said and when she hugged him he felt big and strange.

Putting his hands on her shoulders he kissed her head and said, 'God bless ya.'

Frank reached over and shook her hand awkwardly. He blushed when she reached up and kissed his cheek.

Closing the lid of the boot tightly David looked around but there was no sign of Doireann.

Then they climbed into the car and waved and waved goodbye.

Driving along the road just past the main gates they spotted Doireann standing with Pacha on a grass verge. She beckoned to them to stop. David wound down the window and she moved closer to the car.

'I'm sorry Molly,' she said quietly and with a real sincerity.

Then she leaned into the car and kissed her brother on the cheek. David knew that Doireann was truly sorry for what she had done. He was even more pleased when he heard her whisper to Molly:

'Come back soon won't ya, and maybe we can teach you how to ride.'

'Thanks Doireann,' said Molly as she leaned over and smiled up at her. As they drove away Molly looked back at her. Doireann seemed to be sitting motionless on her horse.

CHAPTER THIRTY FIVE

It was just another typical Sunday afternoon as far as Jessie was concerned, but to J.J. it was very exciting indeed. Kerry were playing Galway in the all Ireland in Croke Park. David and Molly had disappeared after dinner and Jessie was left with the washing up. Not that she minded, she was not going anywhere special. Having read the 'Sunday Press' from cover to cover, J.J. reclined in his armchair and switched on the wireless. He checked the time with his pocket watch and yes everything was going according to plan. Jessie watched him as he folded his newspaper and she thought to herself that he really was a creature of habit.

The familiar voice of Micheal O' Hehir was heard coming over the wireless as he introduced the game. J.J. lit his pipe and lying back in his chair he listened intently to the broadcast.

Fifteen minutes into the game Jessie was just dozing off when she heard the key turn in the lock. Looking up, she was surprised to see David and Molly walk into the room.

Molly was excited about something but poor David looked worried and rather embarrassed.

Molly found it hard to sit still and from time to time and would beam a smile over at David.

Jessie soon twigged as to what was going on.

As the expression on J.J.'s face kept changing according to the score she signalled to the happy couple to sit down and stay quiet until the match went to half time.

Then, at the appropriate moment Molly nudged David and he rose slowly from his seat.

'Em Mr. McDermott, I would like to ask your permission to marry Molly.'

J.J. smiled, and leaning over he tapped his pipe off the side of the fireplace.

'I see,' he said raising an eyebrow, 'and tell me now where would you live?

'Here in Dublin, I will probably buy a house.'

Turning to the two women J.J. said tactfully: ' Jess would you and Molly make us a nice cup of tea please?'

When they women had left the room J.J. continued:

'How soon would you be planning on getting married young man?'

'Well as soon as possible.'

'Sit down there now and tell me what's your hurry.'

'I love Molly and I want to spend the rest of my life with her.'

J.J. stood up and walked over towards the window. After thinking for a few moments, he turned back to David and said:

'Now there's no need for you to go committing yourselves to a house right away. Take your time. You could move into that little flat over the shop while your looking around. That's where Jess and me started ya know.'

Then he began reminiscing: 'Aye, we had many a happy hour in that little flat before we got this place. Jessie took to rearing Molly after her mother died God rest her. I had me doubts then but ya know something over the years I've grown fond of her, very fond of her indeed. Aye she's a good girl and some day I'll leave all this to her.'

Out in the kitchen Molly kept impatiently hovering around Jessie as she tried to set the tea tray.

'Ya know it is nice of David to ask J.J. the way he did,' said Jessie thoughtfully.

'Well he is the only father I've known.'

'Yeah but he's still only your uncle.'

Then a strange dreamy expression spread across Molly's happy face:

'You know something Auntie, I've spent many hours dreaming and thinking about my own father and I suppose in a way that is where he will always be, in my mind. But Uncle J.J. has always been here, here where I could touch him and talk to him. When he told jokes and laughed, I laughed too and when he got sick I was worried in case he might die, And even all those old stories he told over and over again they've come to be part of me now. He has never told me he cares but I see it in his eyes and I feel it in his fingers as he blesses me at night. When I walk up that aisle I want it to be with him. I love him Aunt Jessie.'

Her words went deep into Jessie's heart and she began to see things in a different light. She was also suddenly realizing how Molly felt about her adopted father.

Picking up the tray she said quietly, 'I think we'll go in with the tea now and see what's happening.'

In the sitting room J.J. and David were chatting and laughing beside the window. Molly went over and putting her arms around both their waists, she smiled up happily at the two most wonderful men in her life.

Having been welcomed into the McDermott family with open arms, the following Saturday David took Molly into town to buy an engagement ring. They headed for O'Dowd's jewellery shop on O'Connell Street.

In the large store, the trays of dazzling diamond rings were shining and twinkling behind the clear glass of the long showcases. There seemed too be almost too many to choose from and Molly kept squeezing David's hand excitedly.

After a few moments Molly spotted one on a top tray. the shop assistant handed the ring to her carefully.

'You have a lovely slender finger dear,' she commented as she helped Molly try on the ring for size.

Then David found what he thought was the perfect one. It had three small diamonds set in platinum. Molly tried it on, and it fitted her finger perfectly. The diamonds sparkled in the light as she moved her hand, and she moved her hand quite often.

'Do you like it, darling?' he asked her tenderly.

'Oh yes I do, I really do, it's lovely.'

'Well that's settled then we'll take this one please.'

The shop assistant was caught up in the happiness of the young couple and she wished them well. She gave the ring a final polish with a soft cloth before putting it into the little black box.

David paid her and thanked her and with their arms wrapped around one another they left the shop.

Then he drove straight towards the Phoenix Park and stopped beside their tree. He got out of the car, walked round and opened the door for Molly. Laughing she took his hand and together they ran over to the tree.

David held her close and kissed her.

Taking the ring from the little box he took her left hand and slid it onto her third finger.

'Molly,' he said sincerely, 'When I give you this ring I not only give you my love but I give you my life. You're my girl and nothing will ever part us.'

'Oh David,' she replied, 'I will love you for ever.'

The wind moved in the branches above and sent a shower of autumn leaves confetti-like down upon them.

But they hardly noticed as they kissed, caressed, and loved each other into sheer oblivion.

Chapter Thirty Six

From that September until Christmas David and Molly devoted all their spare time to doing up the flat. David began re-wiring it which meant the whole place had to be redecorated. Molly took extra care with the bathroom and loved the idea of having one all to themselves. From time to time Hattie would arrive with bits of advice, but somehow she always had somewhere to go when anything needed doing.

Molly loved being engaged and when friends and neighbours asked to see the ring she held her hand out with great pride. By Christmas the flat was finished and David went home to Wexford. Molly stayed in Dublin. It was to be their last Christmas as single people and knowing this brought an usual specialness to the season.

Their wedding was set for the 25th May the following year and their friends at the theatre would gather to hear all about the preparations.

In the fish shop Jessie and Hattie could be found chatting and arguing in a very civilized way about final details and Molly and David could only laugh at some of their suggestions.

By February they had booked their reception at one of Dublin's finest hotel's, Jury's on the Green, and for the ceremony they had chosen the beautiful St. Catherine Church on Meath Street. Hattie had offered to help pay for the wedding but J.J. would not hear tell of it. He was careful with his money but his pride was even more precious.

'Molly will have whatever she wants Mrs. Thornton,' he said proudly as he lit his pipe. 'I'll see to that.'

Having sent out the wedding invitations Molly was disappointed when Roseanne wrote and said she could never come back home, not even to be her friends bridesmaid. But she smiled when she opened the wedding gift and she saw a very pretty lace nightdress.

But there was more disappointments to come. Returning from Wexford David looked worried. Frank refused to be bestman as he did not like making speeches while Aggie was afraid to travel as far as Dublin. But Doireann was thrilled to do chief bridesmaid and the Boss was delighted they had asked her. After thinking for a few moments Molly suggested David's friend Matty Duane as best man with Frank doing groomsman. 'Good idea and Seamus's girl Helen can escort Frank,' said David sighing with relief.

The next day Jessie and Molly went into town to buy their wedding clothes. As Jessie hurried through the crowds clutching tightly to her handbag she kept saying to Molly as the young girl stopped to gaze into the windows:

'Come girl, looking at what ya don't want, makes ya buy what ya don't need.'

Deciding to get Jessie's outfit first they headed for Clery's department store. Picking out a Sybil Connolly suit Molly gasped when she saw Jessie wearing it.

'Do you like it Molly? Now I know it's expensive but to hell with it, if I can't splash out now I never will.'

'The colour really suits you,' she replied thinking that she had never seen Jessie so excited about anything.

'I'll take it,' she said to the shop assistant, and once it was packed in the bag she hurried over to the shoe department.

'Maybe you could try a little higher heel,' suggested the assistant.

'Maybe I will Miss,' she said winking at Molly.

Trying on a pair of stiletto's she laughed at the thought of J.J's face when he'd see them.

But in the end she settled for a pair just a little higher than her own.

Then it was on to find a hat. So many shapes and colours to choose from. Deciding on a 'pill box', it sat elegantly on her short permed hair.

'Right that's me done except for a few bits and pieces. Lets go and look at some wedding dresses now.'

But Molly found it difficult to shop with Jessie. She was not relaxed in the shops and Molly could sense it. After a while finding nothing suitable they gave up and caught the bus home.

On the journey back Jessie suddenly turned to Molly and said, 'You know somethin', I think Hattie would be more help to you than me in pickin' out your dress.'

'Oh but....'

'No but's now Molly I know me limits and Hattie knows her shops. So its settled, now you go over and ask her when we get home.'

Feeling very touched by her suggestion Molly replied graciously:
'Thanks Auntie, I think I will.'

So it was Hattie that set off to town with Molly early the next morning.

Walking up the stairs in Brown Thomas Molly suddenly remembered Roseanne.

'Wouldn't she love to be shopping with me today.' she thought sadly.

Then a surge of excitement went through her as they walked over to the bridal department.

Rows and rows of beautiful white and cream dresses hung in mirrored wardrobes. Two shop assistants came to help as Hattie sat down on the couch. She watched Molly glide in and out of the dressing room in one dress lovelier than the next. But only one stood out. It was cream organza, ballet length, with a full skirt. A short veil with a wreath of pretty flowers framed her smiling face.

Looking in the mirror Molly could not believe how beautiful it all looked.

'Yes that is the one,' agreed Hattie.

Then the assistant brought some bridal shoes new in from Paris. Satin covered stilettos with a tiny flower stitched on the base of the toes.

'I feel so tall, I hope I won't fall,' said Molly nervously as she tried to balance in them.

'Well you've plenty of time to practice my dear,' smiled Hattie.

With her trousseau packed in cardboard boxes they all agreed that the bridesmaids would look fabulous in a replica of Molly's dress but in a different colour.

'Yes, well that's another days work,' said Hattie looked at her watch.

For the rest of the afternoon they strolled around the shops and by evening when they returned to No. 28 Molly had almost everything she needed to make her wedding day special.

That evening found her busy in the flat hanging up the last of the new lace curtains.

David was working overtime to make some extra money for their honeymoon. For the first time she heard their door bell ring and hurrying down-stairs she was surprised to see Seamus standing on the

141

doorstep. He was carrying a large oblong box wrapped in wedding paper.

'Hello Molly, is David here?'

'No he's working late, but come on in.'

'Mother sent me round with this present, its from all of us.'

'Oh thanks Seamus,' said Molly excitedly as he carried it upstairs.

'So this is the flat,' he said looking around.

'Not bad.' 'I was just finishing off these curtains when you rang.'

Seamus put the large box on the table and Molly opened it quickly. Putting her two hands in she lifted out a heavy exquisite Waterfordvase. She never had anything so valuable in her whole life and she placed it very carefully on the table. Turning to say thanks to Seamus she realized he was standing quite close to her. Looking deep into her eyes he asked her,

'Are you sure Molly ?'

'Sure of what?' she asked puzzled at his question.

'You and David, this wedding, are you sure?'

'Oh yes, I've never been more sure of anything.

I love him very much and I know we'll be happy.

From the first time I saw him I knew he was the one.'

'You know I was very foolish that morning at our house. I know now I shouldn't have been so insensitive, but I was sure you felt something for me.'

'No Seamus,' she said, stepping to the side, 'both you and William are like family to me.

Maybe that's why I love David so much. He's the father I never knew, the brother I should have had and the husband I always wanted. You were my dear friend in the past Seamus and I hope you always will be in the future.'

Reaching over for a hug he suddenly stopped and pulled out a package wrapped in brown paper from his pocket.

'William asked me to give you this, and he was wondering would you like to carry it instead of a bouquet on your wedding day.'

'What is it,' said Molly as she unwrapped it excitedly.

Then in the next moment, she saw a beautiful ivory covered missal in a matching ivory case. She took it out and turned the pages slowly.

It was the perfect gift from William. Her mind flashed back to the time he declared his love for her on the bridge.

It was one of those moments when a friend who is miles away comes to mind and appears before your eyes.

'Oh Seamus I'll miss him at my wedding, but I know it can't be helped with his ordination so close. Tell him I would be honoured to carry it.'

Seamus hugged her tightly and he knew he was letting go of something very special.

Turning around he made light of the situation by saying in his usual comical way,

'Better let you get back to your curtains. Tell that fella of yours that if he's not good to you he'll have me to reckon with.'

Molly smiled and walked down the stairs with him. Closing the door she raced back up stairs to the flat. Opening the door she caught sight of all her wedding gifts displayed on the table. Leaning against the door she now felt that with all the blessings and love heaped on them by everybody, their future happiness was secure.

CHAPTER THIRTY SEVEN

Molly woke early on the morning of her wedding and while everyone was asleep she tiptoed to the kitchen.

Julie had set her hair in curlers the night before and she had to loosen them as they were starting to hurt. She put the kettle on the cooker and wandered over to the window.

She smiled as she thought about the special day ahead It was as if everything she had ever thought and dreamed about was coming true.

Turning from the window she looked around the kitchen. The clock on the wall tick-tocked in the silence. So much of her childhood had been spent in this kitchen.

She remembered cuddling into Jessie's chest as a child and feeling safe and warm.

She remembered Jessie washing her in a large basin at the cooker. She remembered all the lovely mealtimes sitting round the table and playing and swinging with the thin iron bars underneath. And the more she sat and thought, the more it dawned on her just how much of a good mother Jessie had been.

Then odd feelings of loneliness began creeping in as she remembered more of her childhood

But she was looking forward to her new life with David too, and so all these different feelings running through her were very special indeed.

By the time she had taken her bath J.J. and Jessie were up and about and had her breakfast on the table.

J.J. smiled when he saw her new shoes peeping out from under her dressing gown.

'I'm trying to get used to them,' she said rather nervously.

Patting her affectionately on the shoulder he replied 'It'll be no trouble to ya girl, you'll see.'

After breakfast he decided to get dressed quickly, because he knew that once the women arrived the house would be in utter chaos.

He took extra care shaving and Jessie had all his clothes carefully laid out on the bed. Every item was brand new and it reminded him of his own wedding all those years ago.

A little while later on hearing a knock at the front door he hurried downstairs to answer it.

'Your dressed early aren't you Mr. McDermott,' commented Hattie, as she breezed past him into the kitchen.

'You look very handsome,' said Julie and Doireann, walking in behind nodded her head in agreement.

J.J. smiled proudly to himself as he gave his black silk tie an extra tug.

Jessie led the women upstairs to the bedroom and Julie immediately set about removing the curlers from Molly's hair while Doireann began changing into her bridesmaid's dress.

Hattie sat on the bed in all her finery and went over the details again and again. Julie had to reassure her that everything was going according to plan.

With Molly's hair combed out into a mass of fabulous curls it was time to take her wedding dress out of the tissue paper. Holding up both her arms Doireann slid the gorgeous dress over her head and fastened it at her tiny waist. The short veil with a little spray of flowers was placed on her head, and when she looked in the mirror the women watching her all agreed, that she was indeed a real bride.

Julie turned her attention to Doireann next and when she was dressed she also looked very nice.

Feeling a bit awkward in her bridesmaid's dress, she kept stealing uneasy glances in the mirror.

'You look really beautiful Doireann,' said Molly reassuringly.

'Thanks,' she replied as she blushed.

When the others had left the room Jessie was left alone with Molly. Her eyes roamed from the short veil on her head, up and down her wedding dress and back to her face.

Molly saw tears in her eyes and reached over and gave her a hug.

'I hope you'll be very happy,' she said sincerely.

'Oh we will Aunt Jessie, we will.'

'I really hope so. Now give me a minute or two to get down the stairs. I want to see your uncle's face.'

As Jessie hurried out, Molly's thoughts turned towards her own mother. Glancing over at her parents wedding picture she walked over towards the bed and picked up her missal. Then she took a deep breath and stood very still. Stepping back she looked one more time into the mirror.

In an instant a warm breeze gently lifted her veil and seemed to play with her hair.

Then as she walked down from the top of the wooden stairs J.J. could not take his eyes away.

Reaching out his hand towards her he said thoughtfully: 'I hope David Furlong knows what he's getting.'

Doireann opened the front door and Molly gasped. with delight. For standing outside in the street complete with horse and white rosettes was a beautiful cab.

A small group of neighbours and customers had gathered on the pavement to catch a glimpse of the bride.

The jarvey jumped down from his high seat and tipped his bowler hat as he greeted Molly respectfully.

In his black suit and smart overcoat he stood erect, then reached out to open the door of the cab.

'There's no doubt but that's a fine lookin' cab Mrs. Thornton,' said J.J.

'Cabulette, actually, Mr. McDermott.' She replied proudly and everyone laughed.

As Molly moved closer to it a shy young girl ran over and quickly handed her a flower. It was a poor girl she had often given fish to in the shop.

Before she could thank her she had ran back shyly into the crowd.

Being extra careful not to crush her dress, J.J. sat down beside what he now felt proudly was, his own natural daughter.

'Walk on Darby,' said the jarvey as he flicked the reins and the horse walked slowly from the house.

They wedding procession travelled on past the fish shop and into Meath Street. People waved and cheered as they passed and Molly felt the whole street was rejoicing on her special day.

In St. Catherine's Church David sat nervously in the front seat up at the altar. Beside him the bestman, Matty Duane was no help as he talked on and on about the attractive bridesmaids The guests had taken their seats by the time the cab drew up at the church, and as the jarvey helped Molly down, the first melodic tones of the organ was heard humming softly in the air.

'Best o' luck miss,' he said sincerely once again as he tipped his bowler.

When the photographer had taken his pictures, J.J. and Molly were left alone at the door of the church. He turned to her, and, like so many times before, made the sign of the cross on her forehead. Then holding her arm tightly, they began the long walk up the aisle towards David.

Fr. Brophy smiled encouragingly at them both as they kneeled nervously before him and the ceremony began.

The soprano's golden voice rang through the rafters and filled the church. Then with their friends looking up at them and God looking down on them, David and Molly were married.

Walking out of the Church to a shower of confetti, Mr. and Mrs. Furlong looked radiantly happy. Hattie watched Walter as he threw his arms affectionately around his eldest son's shoulders. The tears welled up in her eyes and she thought back to her wedding with James and Walter's with his Doris.

As her brother moved to one side to congratulate his new daughter-in-law, David suddenly noticed Aggie standing behind him. Reaching out quickly towards her he drew her tightly to his chest.

'Aggie, Aggie,' he said tears welling in his eyes, 'I hoped you'd come.'

'Of course I'd come me boy,' she replied as her frail body trembled with emotion.

Their journey to the hotel was broken only once when they stopped off at the studio, for their special wedding portrait.

Then it was back in the cab and on to Jury's Hotel, College Green. The jarvey pulled the reins and halted the horse.

'Stand easy Darby,' he called sternly.

Then as they were getting out of the cab Hattie ran over and insisted on joining them in a photograph complete with horse and cab.

'This is one for my album,' she said.

Then laughing, Molly and David walked hand in hand into the foyer of the hotel. Dressed in a morning suit the banqueting manager greeted them with two glasses of champagne.

'Would you like to come with me please?' he said courteously as he led the way up the right hand staircase and into the Bohemian Room.

The four tiered wedding cake, with bride and groom on top, sat proudly on the table. The manager showed David and Molly to their seats while the other guests found their own places.

Already seated at the bride's table, Hattie and Jessie were admiring the beautiful lace which adorned the edges of the white linen table cloth.

When everyone was seated Fr. Brophy stood up and said grace and the wedding breakfast was served.

The guests chatted and laughed throughout the three courses and by the time it came round to cutting the three tired cake, there was a lovely atmosphere already in the room.

Molly put her hand gently on top of David's as laughing they plunged the knife into the soft white icing.

Everyone cheered and clapped loudly.

Then the speeches began with Fr. Brophy's spiritual one. J.J. was called on next, and, as he rose from his seat, he pulled a slip of paper nervously from his pocket.

After the usual formalities, he began his speech with these words;

'Molly came into our lives twenty four years ago now, and though Jessie and me reared her, you all know she's not our natural daughter. Looking at her today however I wonder could any daughter have given us more happiness than Molly. David, Jessie and me welcome you into our family and we want you to know your getting a girl in a million. Thank you.'

J.J. sat down to a well deserved round of applause.

Then David was called to speak.

He thanked everyone on behalf of himself and his new wife for their presents and Jessie and J.J. for Molly. He gave a special thanks to Jury's Hotel for the wonderful meal.

Then turning towards his sister Doireann he continued:

'I think Mammy would have been very proud of you today.'

Then he asked everyone to please raise their glasses in a toast for the two beautiful bridesmaids.

When it came to the bestman's speech Matty Duane out did himself with the jokes. He talked about how he knew something fishy was going on with David popping over to McDermott's all the time. How he told him he must have his wires crossed when he mentioned marriage. But he got very suspicious when he found a flower lying between the wires and cable of his van that David borrowed the night before.

Everyone broke their sides laughing and David kept wondering what he was going to come out with next.

But Matty ended his speech very sincerely when he asked everyone to raise their glasses and drink a toast to the bride and groom.

With the speeches over the waitresses cleared the tables and moved them back to make way for the dancing.

David held Molly close for the first romantic number.

Alone on the floor he whispered his love in her ear. She looked up into his wonderful brown eyes and she felt as if her heart would burst with happiness.

Everyone watched them as they waltzed round and round the floor. Then for the next dance they were joined by Doireann, Matty, Frank and Helen. Soon everyone was dancing and the wedding party was in full swing.

A little while later David stood chatting and laughing with Matty at the bar. A waiter came up and, pulling him to one side, told him that an old man wanted to speak to him out on the street. But he must come alone. Puzzled as to who it might be he excused himself and made his way quickly down the stairs towards the main door.

Once outside he looked left and right. Suddenly, he noticed an old man peering out from the corner of the building. He beckoned to him and David approached him cautiously.

'Are you alone?' the man asked as he looked suspiciously around.

David nodded.

'Ya don't know me... I'm Mick McCoy, Molly's father, I've come to warn ya.'

Though he was very shocked at his new found father-laws antics David managed to say amusedly.

'Warn me about what?'

'Ya must listen ta me now,' he continued seriously, 'for she must never have a child.'

'Who are you talking about?' asked David confusedly.

'Molly, yer bride, if she has a child she'll die.'

A fear suddenly gripped David.

'How do you mean die?' he asked angrily

'Now I've come a long way to warn ya and ya must listen to me. A child will kill her like it did her mother and all them before.'

'What the hell are you goin' on about? Said David getting more agitated.

'Oh I know what I'm talkin' about alright, and you better heed me, do ya hear me now?' and he turned to walk away.

David stepped forward and roughly pulled him back.

'No, don't go, Molly would want to see you, especially today,' he said anxiously.

Mick turned and with sad eyes looked back at the hotel. Then in a moment his expression changed and a blank stare came over his face.

Looking up at David he said crossly, as he jerked free of his grip,

'No I don't want to see the child.'

Watching the weary thin figure scurry away, the full implication of the old man's words slowly dawned on him. He turned back into the hotel and walked slowly through the foyer and up the stairs. Deep in thought, he was barely aware of friends coming up to greet him. Standing at the door of the Bohemian Room he watched Molly as Seamus twirled her round on the floor. He thought how magnificent she looked. If what he had just heard was true then it was dreadfully unfair.

Catching sight of her new husband Molly smiled. Unable to return that smile he just managed to give a little wave.

For it was now he realised that he would have to protect her from the one thing he wanted to share with her, full and intimate passion.

CHAPTER THIRTY EIGHT

The night they returned home from their honeymoon Molly lay in bed beside David and watched him sleeping. She stroked his hair gently and the tears rolled silently down her cheeks. She knew that he loved her but that was not enough. Her body was crying out to express that love and yet there was little or no response from him. She looked up to heaven.

'Why?' she asked herself, 'Oh why?'

As she lay thinking and crying she knew she would have to talk to someone.

'I know, I will go and see Hattie, she's his aunt, she will know what's wrong.'

As soon as David left for work Molly took out her bike and cycled over to number 28.

She hesitated a little then knocked on the door.

Julie was surprised to see her.

'Why hello there Molly,' she said 'what brings you round here so early?'

'Oh nothing really, I've just come for a chat.'

'Did you have a good time on your honeymoon?'

'Yeah it was nice.'

Noticing a sadness in her eyes Julie took her arm and gently pulled her inside.

'Mrs. Thornton doesn't usually talk to anyone this hour of the morning.'

'Maybe I'll call back later' said Molly as she turned for the door.

'Nonsense, you go right up there and chat all you like. That's just what she needs, and by the way, when your finished give me a shout and I'll bring up her breakfast.'

'Thanks Julie,' said Molly as she tiptoed up the stairs.

Once outside Hattie's bedroom door she hesitated as she hoped the older woman would not be angry with her for waking her up. But then she had to knock several times on the door before Hattie's voice could be heard telling her to come in.

'Leave the light Julie, it hurts my eyes.'

'It's not Julie, it's me, Molly,'

'Oh I thought you were Julie. What time is it? Come in dear.'

Molly walked slowly to the side of the four -poster bed and sat down.

Putting her hand up dramatically to her forehead Hattie complained:

'I feel so down today Molly, I haven't the energy to move. But for that silly busman blowing his horn I would still be asleep.'

'Will I come back later?'

'No, No, dear, you just sit quietly on the side of the bed now and tell me all about your honeymoon. How's that lovely husband of yours?'

Molly said nothing. Noticing her silence Hattie asked:

'Is something the matter dear?'

'No, well not really.'

'What do you mean not really?'

'It's nothing, it's stupid.'

Hattie took her hand down from her forehead.

'Come Molly, if there's a problem you must say.'

'Well, it's David... No it's not him... it's me.'

Getting frustrated with her riddles Hattie said impatiently;

'Well which of you is it then? I hope he is not being unkind to you.'

'Oh no, nothing like that,' she said jumping to his defence. 'David loves me, at least I think he does.'

'Think he does!' exclaimed Hattie in astonishment and with that she sat up in the bed.

'What exactly do you mean when you say you think he does?'

Molly did not reply and started crying instead.

Sensing something was dreadfully wrong

Hattie grew more sympathetic and said caringly:

'My dear, don't cry, things can't be that bad. Why you're just home from your honeymoon and you're probably a little tired after the fuss and bother of it all.'

'No Hattie that's not it, I think there is something wrong with me.'

By now Hattie was wide awake. She got out of bed and sat beside Molly. Holding her hand she asked worriedly, 'Have you seen a doctor?'

'Oh no, it's nothing like that. David ... well... he won't... he doesn't seem to want to...'she blurted out and burst out crying again.

'Want to what Molly ?'

'He won't make love to me,' she said.

Hattie was stunned. What could she say? She rose from the bed and walked towards the window. She pulled back the curtains, then returned and sat beside a weeping Molly. She listened intently as she blurted out all the sorry details of her honeymoon in between sobbing and weeping.

'It must be my fault,' she said, 'maybe I'm not pretty enough.'

Hattie grew rather angry at this remark and reached for her cigarettes.

'What do you mean you are not pretty enough? You know your pretty. No, it can't be that. There was certainly nothing wrong with his father in that department. I shall have to get to the bottom of this. Maybe I should have a talk with him.'

'Oh no Hattie.' said Molly, horrified at the idea 'I would die if you mentioned this to David. This is private between him and me, I'm only telling you because I don't know what else to do.'

'Now calm down Molly, I won't say a word I promise.'

Hattie pulled hard on her cigarette as she walked up and down the room. It was hard to think with Molly sobbing. She looked at her sitting there, so young, so innocent. Completely inexperienced in the ways of men. Well she, Hattie, would have to tell her exactly what she should do.

She sat down beside her and began: 'Now Molly, dry your eyes and listen to me please. You love David don't you?'

'Yes, with all my heart.'

'Good, and he loves you, yes.'

Molly nodded in agreement.

'So, my girl, I want you to go home, and when the time is right you must be the one to approach him. You must show him how much you love him. There is a power that every woman has Molly, use it, and he will not be able to resist you. You must kiss him, and caress him. Maybe put on some exotic perfume to heighten his desire, but go to him Molly and find his love, for it is yours to have. Whatever reason it is hidden, you must be the one to bring it to the surface.

Then she choked a little as she recalled a regretted memory.

'If James were here today I would not waste a second of love. It's so precious. Molly go to him, and together you will find it.'

'Oh Hattie, do you really think so,' she said hopefully.

'I know so,' she replied and the two women embraced each other.

'I'm sorry to be troubling you with my problems,' said Molly.

'Not at all, isn't that what I'm here for.'

Then looking over at the clock she said;

'Anyway its high time I was up and about. Julie is late with the breakfast, she must have went back to bed. I shall have to speak to her.'

But Molly was not listening at all. Hattie's advice was going round and round in her head and she desperately needed to go home.

'I better leave now Hattie,' she said rising from the bed,' and thanks for everything.'

As she left the room Hattie smiled to herself.

Then in a rather mischievous way she called after her:

'Let me know how you got on dear,'

Molly blushed and ran down the stairs. She almost knocked Julie down in the hallway.

'Hattie's ready for her breakfast now,' she said smiling,' and Julie,

'Yes Molly,'

'I have a feeling it's going to be a lovely day.'

CHAPTER THIRTY NINE

Arriving back at the flat all the worry and tension of the past two weeks had disappeared and new feelings of love and determination had taken their place. Looking around Molly knew she had a lot to do before David returned that evening. She set about cleaning and arranging the rooms, taking extra care with the bedroom. She thought deeply about Hattie's advice. It was funny but she would never have made the first move towards love-making. In all the romantic novels she'd read it was always the man who made the advances.

Molly had always dreamed of being swept off her feet. She knew David had been aroused by her kisses and yet he always seemed to be the one to break off. Well tonight she would summon up all her feelings and he would not resist, tonight would be different.

By twelve noon she had finished cleaning and was sitting on the edge of the bed counting her money. It totalled two pounds and ten shillings, that was plenty. Molly was going shopping. She called into the fish shop on the way.

It was very thoughtful of Jessie to give her two weeks off work to settle into the flat and have a little more time with David.

'I'm going into town if you want anything,' she inquired, popping her head round the door.

'Oh would you get me a pound of Hafners sausages, there's a good girl.' said Jessie as she opened the till and gave her the money.

'Are you getting anything nice for yourself?'

'Oh just some perfume,' she replied but then unknown to herself she blushed.

'Well I won't keep you then,' said Jessie, 'See you later.'

When she was gone Jessie smiled to herself. It was easy to see that Molly was still on her honeymoon.

Walking around the perfume counter she found it hard to choose from all the wonderful fragrances. Picking out a bottle of 'lily of the valley' the shop assistant remarked:

'Your young man will like this one,' she said, noticing the shiny new rings on Molly's left hand.

Smelling the enchanting vapour, Molly replied excitedly, 'Oh I hope so.'

With the bottle safely in her bag she walked quickly down the street. Passing the flower sellers she found them hard to resist and stopped and bought a bunch of pink carnations.

It had been the quickest trip she ever made to town and there was only three hours until David returned home.

Arriving back she raced upstairs and entering the kitchen she turned on the gas boiler to heat the water.Then, after arranging the flowers in a vase, she placed them on the bedside locker.

Now what would they have for the evening meal? Salad, that was it. She did not want to steam the place up with the smell of cooking.

As she prepared the salad she sang her favourite song, 'When Irish eyes are smiling.'

But later while soaking in the bath she found that doubts were starting to creep into her mind.

What would she do if she was rejected? That would be terrible. She would hide her love and it would be a long time before she could ever give it again. Then negative thoughts such as these would be suddenly taken over by more positive ones. She lay back in the lavender-scented water and smiled as she remembered that wonderful day in 'Paradise'. Then she began thinking about the night ahead.

When David arrived home he saw that she had gone to a lot of trouble to make the flat nice and he gave her a big kiss. But as she watched him eat his meal it took all her self control to suppress her love and excitement.

'I've had a hard day Molly,' he said stretching his arms, 'these old houses are no joke to wire I can tell you. I will have to soak in the bath. Is the water hot?'

'No,' she said impatiently, 'I will have to switch it on again.'

By the time the water was hot and David had retired to the bathroom Molly was getting nervous and unsure of herself.

While he whistled his tunes she went into the bedroom and got undressed. She put on the beautiful lace nightdress Roseanne had given her for her trousseau. Moments later when David stepped into the room, Molly was standing in front of the lamp. Looking through the almost transparent material of her nightdress, his eyes excitedly traced every curve of her sensuous body and went very slowly back to her lovely face. He had only seen that particular look in her eyes once before and he instinctively knew now that she wanted him.

Standing before him, she also knew that the desire in his eyes was for her and her alone. For the first time she experienced the real glory of her own sexuality. She could almost feel his skin without touching it and the sense of his masculinity excited her.

She dropped her gaze to his hands. They were large and hairy and strong as only a man's hands can be.

The need to be caressed by these hands seemed to burn deeply within her.

'I will be loved,' her thoughts almost cried out,' I need to be loved. I have waited such a long time.'

She moved closer towards him slipping her nightdress teasingly from her shoulders, dropping it slowly to her hips until it slithered sensuously down her long legs and rested at her feet.

David urgently discarded the bath towel and lay down naked on the bed and as he watched her beauty unfold before his eyes he groaned, 'Oh Molly.'

Like every woman in love her movements naturally took on an erotic form as she crept cat-like on to the bed beside him. Her dilated eyes bore deep into his.

Her desire and longing for him was burning in every muscle and sinew. Her freshly washed hair, featherlike, fell as snowflakes over her shoulders and framed hertiny face. It brushed against his skin as shemoved even close. ' Molly I ...' he protested.

But his words were immediately silenced by a passionate kiss. Lips that were soft and warm came down on his as Molly's love was unleashed.

He tried hard to resist and for a moment it seemed as if he was winning as he held her tightly, but her perfume drifted into his nostrils and he found he was now lost in her kisses.

Molly intertwined her slender fingers in his and pulled his hands up over his head and in one determined movement she matched her body on top of his until the two blended perfectly into one.

The softness of her lovely white skin amazed him as it felt like velvet to his touch.

'Oh Molly, you are a real woman and I love you,' he moaned as she moved and swayed and pressed and touched him. Then in an instant he was gone, gone past the point where lovers step over that invisible line into a world of sheer magic and excitement.

His passion was now stronger than hers and her lips knew no boundaries as they discovered his secrets. Realising that he was now as crazy to be loved as she, Molly lay down freely and relaxed in his arms.

Then as he gently pushed his love into her she knew she that her very existence was complete.

There was no clock. There was no time.

There was just David and Molly.

Lying together after the shock and wonder of it all, their breathing was quick and their bodies tingling.

Molly held David as he lay in ecstasy on her soft breasts and, stroking his lovely black hair, she whispered into his ear,

'Oh David, you are mine and nobody will ever love you like I do.'

CHAPTER FORTY

At five a.m. Mrs. B. Fawlor picked up the telephone beside her bed and spoke like a general directing her troops:

'Are you ready?'

'Yes we are,' came the reply from her staff and with that her travelling kitchens left her hotel in Naas.

A fleet of red lorries with green canvas tops began its journey along the winding road to Maynooth.

Down in Wexford the Furlong's had also risen early, in order to make good time for the two hour journey to Maynooth. They would only make one stop and that was to pick up Aggie Cullen at her cottage.

She was dressed in her Sunday coat and hat and they waited patiently while she hugged each one of her cats before getting in the car.

Up in Dublin, Hattie was in her usual state of organised panic. She had poor Julie running around in circles. David and Molly walked over from their flat and joined the family just as they were about to get into the car. On the journey to Maynooth, Hattie wanted to hear all about their honeymoon, and as David recalled the happy event Seamus noticed his mother's mind was wandering. He knew she was getting nervous about today, and that she really hoped it would pass without a hitch. Reassuringly, he reached over and squeezed her hand.

At the college there was an air of excitement as the seminarians looked forward to meeting their families and friends.

Just as the last of the catering lorries had unloaded the food, tableware and wine, the first of the cars began arriving at the main gates.

The magnificent chapel in the college was decorated with wonderful scented flowers and white candles.

For seven years the class of '59 had been working towards this very special day . Ninety-five young men had started the course, but only forty-five had finished.

A feeling of great anticipation was evident as the young men walked the long spacious corridors of the college.

For one young seminarian, however, the build-up to his ordination could only be compared to a bridegroom on his wedding day.

William Thornton was full of joy. He had a feeling of being special and this was confirmed by the reverence shown to him by the people.

His heart was full of love for mankind and he felt as if he could embrace the whole world.

Each priest was allowed ten guests at his table and Hattie, Seamus, Julie, Frank, Walter, Doireann, Aggie, David and Molly were only too delighted to accept the invitation.

They arrived at the chapel early, as Hattie wanted a seat with a good view of the altar.

However, when they entered the church they found that these seats were already allotted.

Then the choir began its heavenly chorus and the procession began.

During the solemn ceremony William lay prostrated at the Bishop's feet. Extending his hands over William's head, the Bishop invoked the Holy Spirit to descend upon the young man's soul. At that moment the presence of the Divine Love caused a very spiritual union between Jesus Christ and William. From now on Father Thornton would become a mediator between heaven and earth, and from the altar he would bring to the people the bread of life. Of his own free will, William had became a priest forever.

Finding it all extremely moving, his mother, Hattie looked up at the magnificent stained glass windows. It was not merely her motherly emotions that were gathering in her chest, it was not the happy feeling of joy to see William so virtuous at such a young age. As her eyes filled with tears she knew that this was a time of much deeper feelings. It was the fulfilment of the prayer she had said at his baptism.

Molly squeezed David's hand remembering their own wedding day. She suddenly realised how deep William's faith really was. It was easy for her to love David, he was standing beside her.

But William was dedicating his life to someone he had never seen. As the forty-five seminarians prayed together a feeling of great power went up in the church. After the ceremony they all gathered in the large garden. William's friend and classmate Fr. Harold Byrne came over to him and the two young priests shook hands eagerly. Then the Thornton family knelt at William's feet to receive his first blessing. The photographer motioned to Hattie and she stood proudly beside her son in her new suit and matching hat.

Then Hattie invited Julie and Aggie to stand in with them for the next one, and to any stranger passing by it would have been hard to know exactly which one was William's mother. Then everyone took their place for a group shot.

Later as they made their way to the refectory Molly had a chance to show William some of her wedding photographs.

'They are really lovely,'. he said 'and you looked beautiful. Are you happy Molly?' he asked caringly.

'Yes, William, I am,' she replied and looking into her lovely eyes filled with happiness, he had no reason to doubt her words.

Entering the refectory, Hattie and Julie were absolutely amazed to see solid silver cutlery gleaming on the white linen tablecloths.

Delicate china of 'Indian Tree' pattern held white serviettes bearing the Fawlor crest. Crystal glasses sparkled in the daylight and, as the head waiter showed them to their seats, everyone marvelled at the beauty and attention to detail of each table setting.

After grace was said by Bishop Darwin McDaid, waiters in black suits appeared with bowls of soup hopped along their arms; moving with military precision they never spilled a drop. Then waitresses in black and white uniforms joined them to serve the main course. During the meal William informed his guests that this was the refectory where they usually had their meals.

'We are not allowed to talk amongst ourselves at meal times as one of the lads reads from scripture. Then he smiled, 'today, however, is an exception, I'm afraid I've been picked to speak on behalf of my classmates.'

'Well it won't be the first time we had to listen to one of your sermons,' said Seamus jokingly.

Hattie scowled at him from underneath the brim of her hat.

When the dinner plates were cleared away the waiters reappeared carrying large silver bowls.

Standing on four legs in the centre of the table the bowls held Fawlor's famous trifle.

As the guests helped themselves in silence, everyone laughed as Walter and Seamus reached for the serving spoon at the same time. When the coffee and tea cups arrived, Aggie was further amazed to see Walter's big hand trying to come to terms with the dainty china coffee cup. As the Dean arose from his seat to introduce Fr. William Thornton a hush came over the crowd. Touching his mother's shoulder as he passed, William walked over to the microphone and began to speak.

'My Lord, Reverend Fathers, ladies and gentlemen, you are all very welcome to Maynooth today for the ordination of the class of '59. I wish to welcome especially our parents, and to thank them for the many sacrifices they have made in order for their sons to be ordained. And also for your support and love down through the years. May God bless and keep you always .'He paused as the priests broke out
in tremendous applause for their parents.
William smiled down at his mother.
Then a hush came over the crowd and he continued to speak.

'As I prepared for this special day I wondered what I should speak about, and having thought of many things, one kept returning to me time and time again. I knew then that I would have to speak, not just about the priest, but about the man that you see standing before you.

Today I have given up many things. Among them the right to have children and the joy of a wife. These would have been very precious to me. So as I look around this gathering today, I wish to speak from my heart to the men here present.'
He paused for a moment and then continued,
'Although we are men, I speak as if we were not.
I refer to our spirits and not to our forms.
For men seek perfection, but are themselves imperfect.
We walk by trees and we do not see them.
We hold our children and we do not feel them.
We love women but we never take the time to know them.
The unobtainable excites us and makes us reckless, and we become incapable of seeing. But I will tell you now, that until we recognise our own imperfections we will not find what we seek. We must open our hearts and lay them bare. We must search through our emotions until our insides become our outsides and nothing is hidden. We must be humble of heart, and our veil of blindness will be lifted.

Only then will we see life through God's eyes. Our hearts will come back to our beginnings and our needs will be fulfilled by our goodness and not by our greed.

162

Then will our real lives begin.

We will find courage of convictions and we will know what is worth having and what we must throw away. And as we battle with daily life, these great truths shall be our weapons against the stupidity of other men.

'We have a power,
We have a strength,
And we are the leaders.

But it is not until we truly love that we are made in the image of God.'

Everyone was touched by Williams words and applauded loudly. As he made his way back to his seat, Walter leaned over to Hattie and whispered,

'You must be a very happy woman today.'

'Oh yes,' she replied, touching his arm affectionately, 'and you know Walter, today is one of those days when I can't help feeling that James is quite near to me.'

Archbishop Darwin McDaid eyed the assembled gathering during the prayer of thanksgiving. So it was not by chance that he came down the dining room on the left hand side. Looking along the rows he stopped beside William. As he extended his hand towards him, his pale lips asked: 'Did I get your name son?'

Rising quickly from his seat William got down on one knee and taking his Lorships hand, he muttered nervously into the Bishop's ring.

'William Thornton, your grace.'

'You left out authority and obedience,' the Bishop said sternly, as he moved away.

Taken aback, William anxiously resumed his seat.

'Well I hope you never grow into one of them Willie,' said Seamus as he scowled after the Bishop.

Looking across at his mother, William's face relaxed and resumed it's natural colour. He did not reply but his eyes spoke volumes.

CHAPTER FORTY ONE

The wipers on the red Volkswagen could barely clear the heavy rain from the windscreen as David drove towards Wexford. He drove quite fast on the twisting roads with the darkness of the evening closing in. The weather only added to his terrible feelings of fear and guilt.

He could still see, in his minds eye, Molly's face as she told him that she was expecting their child.

At first he thought she was mistaken, it could not have happened so quickly. But when she told him it had been confirmed by Dr. Wilson he knew his greatest fear had come true.

There was only one person he could talk to about this. One person who knew all about curses and folklore and herbs and healing.

It was dark as the lights of the car picked out the wooden gate in their beams. Stopping the engine he got out of the car quickly and hurried up the path.

The cottage had a welcoming glow of candlelight but there was no response to his knocking.

Raising the latch he walked into the kitchen calling Aggie's name. A familiar old voice answered him back. Following her hoarse voice it led him to a small room off the kitchen. In the candlelight he could just about make out her small frame sitting up in bed. Her white hair, which was usually tied up in a bun, was spread out like fine wool on the pillow.

Her wrinkled old hands trembled and pulled embarrassingly at the neck of her nightie as she held it under her chin.

Looking around the room he noticed an old wardrobe that the boss had thrown out years ago. He never knew where it had gone until now. It, and the bed were the only bits of furniture in the small room, while a chair served as a locker beside the bed.

'Oh, Master David, is there anythin' wrong? Is it the Boss? she asked worriedly.

'No, he's fine Aggie,' said David catching hold of her hand. Its nothing like that...I just need to talk to you.'

'Well thank God for that. Is Molly with ya?'

'No, I came alone.'

'Well bring a chair from the kitchen and sit with me awhile. I have this terrible cold and it doesn't seem to be shiftin'.

David went to get the chair while Aggie pulled a black woolly shawl tightly around her shoulders.

'So, Molly's not with ya, ya say.'

'No Aggie, Molly's in Dublin, but she sends her love.'

'Such a beautiful bride, what a great day it was.'

'Yes it was, wasn't it,' he replied wistfully.

And what would ya make of Hattie? Did ya see her in all her finery. Shur, she was never one to denude herself in anything but the finest of clothes.'

'She looked well alright, and I was glad that you made the journey, it meant a lot to us Aggie.'

'Aye, and I'm glad I went,' she said patting his hand.

'So tell me now, what is it that brings a young man like you to visit an old woman on a cold damp night?'

He began telling her about Mick McCoy turning up at the reception and his warning to him.

Then he told her that Molly was pregnant and how he was worried sick that she might die.

'Can there be such curses on people Aggie?'

The old woman thought for a few moments and whispered:

'Did ya tell anyone else about this?'

'No, I haven't. At first I tried to ignore it as an old fool's ramblings but then I thought if it were true there would be dreadful consequences. Oh Aggie, tell me there can be no such curse.'

Reaching behind her pillow she pulled out a small crucifix and blessed herself. Then turning towards him she said:

'I've lived a long time now and I've seen life.

I can't read nor write, but thank God I can see. There's folk who curse the good and hurt the innocent but they've never known real love. From what you've told me it seems as if Molly's father only loved himself. Life can be cruel ya know, with its twists and turns. When her mother died shur his loss was great, but his mistake was even greater. They talk about the bravery of men in battle. When they come home they heap medals and honours on them. But ya know somethin' David?'

√hat's that Aggie?'

'The real bravery in this world is the people who stay. Like your father, the Boss. When the Mistress died, his pain knew no end, but instead of runnin' he turned all that grief into happiness.

Everyday he got up and gave himself to yez all.'

'I never thought of it like that,' said David, 'he was always so quiet and unassuming .'

'Ah hah,' said Aggie, 'ya see, evil goes round shoutin' and makin' a great noise, but love lies as quiet as a lamb. Then when life calls, it becomes a great force. Go back to yer lass master David and give her all the love ya can.'

'But she has my love already, will it be enough?'

Aggie smiled and looked deep into his eyes.

'Ah Master David, love, real love, is honest, it's not keepin' secrets. It's sharin' yer deepest thoughts, yer greatest fears. It's being able to let someone look into your heart. When ya have this love ya must share it, ya must give it.'

Realising that feeling love was not enough David asked Aggie, 'But how can I do this?'

'You must tell 'er, you must show 'er. By the way you look at her. Reaching over she took David's strong hands in her wrinkled old ones 'Hold her and touch her.'

Turning his hands upwards she raised her gaze and looked deeper into his eyes.

'Every man can touch with the palms of his hands but few have the power to feel a response with their fingers.'

As if he knew exactly what she meant he nodded in agreement. Then letting go of his hands she just lay back exhausted on the many pillows.

'Ya must think these things out on your journey home. Molly will deliver yer child safely

I've no doubt, but whether she lives or dies that's in the hands of the Lord. All you have is time David. Use it to love Molly.'

The wind and rain continued to beat noisily on the window panes and David and Aggie talked and talked. Eventually he noticed she was getting tired. He went to leave.

'I'm not calling to the house, Aggie, so don't tell anyone I was here.'

'Ah sur stay with me another while then and we'll have a cup of tea...don't ya worry now son, I'll tell no one.'

David made the tea and brought it in on a tray.

Aggie took the warm cup in her cold hands and welcomed it gladly. Then he said goodbye and left for home. On the way back to Dublin David thought long and hard about all that Aggie had told him. He believed she was right and he was going home to do just that.

In the days and months that followed, his thoughts were completely tied up with Molly and their unborn child. He realised that their love was the most important thing in his life. Their lovemaking became frequent and very passionate and Molly's response convinced him that Aggie was right.

The winter evenings grew shorter and the dark nights grew longer. Molly was amazed at how her figure changed from month to month.

Despite a few mornings sickness, her pregnancy settled down and she enjoyed good health. Feeling a bit tired after her day's work in the shop, she loved to relax on the couch in the evening.

David would sit on a large cushion placed on the floor beside her and they talked for hours about their life, thoughts and hopes. As they chatted their minds entered into each other's worlds and a greater understanding and appreciation rose up between them.

David's work had increased as more building went on in Dublin. Both he and Matty worked hard but he turned down any overtime as he needed to be home with Molly. At this time his day took on a whole new meaning, and work just seemed to be a distraction from where he really wanted to be. He walked by pubs in the evening and wondered how the men inside drinking couldn't go home. Could so many not have love waiting for them, or was it that they were blind to what they had.

Walking through the park, it was as if he was seeing nature for the first time. The urgency he had before to get things done was gone.

Instead, a great calmness and peace entered his soul. The days seemed longer and it was as if he could slow time down. He watched people hurry about their business and all the while he smiled. He had gone beyond that. Before he had lived to work, now he was working so Molly and him could live. He wanted to buy her things and make her happy. When she smiled his heart turned over. He found that the more he gave of himself the more he had to give. Love was endless.

Their happiness spilled over to their friends and family as they all awaited the birth of the baby.

At last the dark days of winter were over and spring arrived with all its freshness. The days lengthened and the sun grew warmer. Molly was quite helpless now as the birth grew nearer but she did not mind. Every day was nearer to one of the most important days of her life.

CHAPTER FORTY TWO

The fishing boats were tied up fast in Howth Harbour. The radio was sending out storm warnings all morning. The wind moved the boats like a cat playing with a mouse, not yet ready to deliver the final blows.

J.J. McDermott stood in the doorway of his shop. Looking up at the angry dark, cloud- filled sky, he decided it would be safer to stay at home today and not travel on his fish round. As for Molly, she lay tucked up in bed cosy and warm. Her hand caressed her swollen tummy and the baby responded. Its limb moved quickly beneath her stretched skin. There was only two weeks until the birth, and gazing up at the sky through the window, she tried to imagine what the baby might look like.

David, sitting on the bedside, was putting on his socks when Molly reached over and took his hand.

Placing it on her tummy, they smiled at each other when they felt their child move.

'I think you would be safer staying indoors today Molly,' said David as he finished dressing.

'I have a job in Fitzwilliam Square and I should be back about 1 p.m. so we can think of something to do for the evening.'

Putting his arms around her he looked down at her sleepy face and tousled hair. He still marvelled at the fact that his woman could sometimes look just like a little girl.

'I love you, Molly,' he said tenderly.

'Oh David, I love you too.' and they kissed a long and gentle kiss.

As soon as David had gone to work, Molly put her breakfast tray down on the floor and struggled to sit up.

Pulling back the sheets she decided she would have to do something today. She felt so well, so full of energy, why, she had not felt like this for a long time.

After washing and dressing she set about cleaning the bedroom. She sang as she worked.

How she loved the smell and feel of fresh aired sheets on the bed. She took her new clothes from the drawer and held them up to her ɔody. She could not wait to wear them again, she was so fed up of the maternity ones.

An hour later she was finished her task and bent down to pick up David's slippers. Suddenly the first strong contraction hit Molly and, instinctively clutching her tummy, she fell back against the bed. Her belly felt hard as the muscles tightened.

When the pain passed she continued to clean the room, but with the next pain her legs gave way and she fell to the floor.

Unaware of how flushed her face had become, Molly looked up helplessly at the clock.

'David won't be home for another two hours,' she thought and suddenly two hours seemed forever.

Then she decided to get up off the floor and to lie on the bed. As the pains came and went, frightened tears trickled down her face.

She knew if she shouted for Jessie, her Aunt would never hear her.

'Oh David hurry home,' she cried.

When he eventually arrived back and opened the bedroom door, David knew at a glance that his wife was not well. He ran over to her and asked nervously:

'Molly, is it the baby?'

Biting hard on her bottom lip she nodded.

'Right, I'm going for the doctor, don't worry Molly, everything will be alright.'

Running quickly down the stairs, he ran into the fish shop.

'But the baby's not due for another fortnight,' said Jessie as she took in his anxious words.

With a surprised look on her face, she quickly took off her soiled apron, and locked the shop.

Then she headed in one direction while David headed off in another.

The note on the dispensary door stated that Dr. Wilson had been called out, and in case of an emergency, patients were to go to the hospital.

David stood thinking for a moment, and in his panic he decided Molly was in too much pain to be shifted.

'But Molly needs a doctor now,' he thought anxiously. Then he remembered Seamus, wasn't he home on holidays, why, he had delivered babies before.

He kept knocking frantically on the door of number twenty eight, and when Julie eventually answered it, he raced past her into the hall, shouting for Seamus. Both Hattie and Seamus appeared at the same time and when they had made sense of David's breathless words, Seamus grabbed his bag and they all piled into the car and headed back to Molly.

It was a very distressed young woman that Seamus saw when he walked into the bedroom.

Molly's hair was stuck to her face with perspiration, her cheeks were red and flushed. Taking her hand to feel her pulse, Seamus said in a comforting voice;

'Listen to me Molly, you have brought the baby this far, it's up to us now. I'll look after you.' Molly smiled gratefully up at him.

Then Jessie and David left the room while he examined her. When he rejoined them on the landing a few minutes later, he told them he had broken the waters and Molly's labour should progress quite normally.

'Is she going to be alright?' asked David in a worried voice.

'Yes, she is, I have done this sort of thing before you know. Now, go and wait down in the kitchen with mother, please and Jessie, would you fetch some towels, disinfectant and warm water.'

As he entered the kitchen David hardly heard a word that Hattie and J.J. were discussing. He just sat down slowly on the chair, placing his hands together he bowed his head and prayed silently;

'God help us,' he pleaded.

By now Molly's contractions had become one continuous long pain. Her breathing had become quick and anxious as she lay moaning and suffering as only a woman in labour can know. Outside the strong gusts of wind rattled the glass, and the gentle breeze, which usually comforted her, seemed to be lost in the volume of the gusts outside. Soon it was as if her pains and the storm had became one. As she lay listening to the storm she felt as if her very being was been torn apart by a force stronger than the world. Crying out in torment Jessie, holding her hand to comfort her, heard her say,

'Oh I wish the storm would stop, it's frightening me.'

Jessie continued to wipe Molly's forehead with a facecloth, while Seamus sat at the foot of the bed keeping watch for signs of the baby.

Downstairs David paced the floor as the time went slowly by. He felt so helpless. Why did she have to suffer so? He would make it up to her.

Oh it was all his fault anyway. He should have been more careful. But how can love be careful.

Love is mad, love is crazy. Can a starving man be asked not to eat? His mind flashed back to Molly standing before him, her eyes full of love, wanting him. She was in his veins and he only came alive in her arms.

Upstairs Seamus looked at his watch. If the baby did not make an appearance soon he would have to move Molly to Holles Street hospital.

Just then, they saw what he was waiting for.

'I can see the baby's head, now Molly, I want you to summon up all your energy and push hard. Come on, you've done so well up to now.

Just another little bit to go.'

Molly pushed and with enormous effort her baby gushed forth and slid into Seamus's capable hands. As he held it up she noticed that it was a blue-black colour, not dead and not alive either, in a world of transit.

'It's a girl,' said Seamus, his voice breaking with emotion. Suddenly the baby let out a forceful cry. It's skin turned a healthy pink colour of life.

On hearing the cry Molly gave a great sigh of relief and said:'Is she alright?'

'Yes dear she's perfect.'

Jessie, still apprehensive, looked on in silence.

'Look Auntie, she's the image of David,' said Molly as Seamus laid the warm baby by her side.

Stroking the little head of black hair Jessie replied:

'You've been a very brave girl, but you must rest now, I'll go and tell David he has a daughter.'

Catching Jessie's hand Molly whispered her thanks and Jessie leaned forward and kissed her cheek.

'Give me a few minutes here,' said Seamus.

'I'll call you when I'm ready.'

When Jessie had left the room, he began to take care of Molly's needs.

Molly lay in bed caressing the baby's fingers and delighting in the wonderful aroma of new birth.

'I think the storm is over.' remarked Seamus and as they both listened they were aware of a great calmness in the room.

'I'm glad it was you here, Seamus, and not old Doctor Wilson. I feel safer with you,' said Molly happily.

'Well, I hope you never call me 'Old Doctor Thornton' he replied with a broad smile.

'No you will always be 'young Doctor Thornton' to me,' and her smile was reflected in her eyes.

Suddenly and without warning the wind rose up and rippled the sheets, Seamus looked towards the window but the window was fastened tight. Returning to his task he felt a strong breeze on the back of his neck. Glancing towards the door he was suddenly pushed back against the bed and the wind blew stronger. An eerie feeling crept over him. Like a bolt from the past, he remembered the wind in the classroom all those years ago. Holding tightly to the bedpost he became very aware of another presence in the room. Raising his arms to shield his eyes from the wind, he failed to see Molly sit up and stare at something above him. Only Molly could see and hear her mother standing there. Dressed in spotless white she looked young and beautiful just as she had on her wedding day. Her ghostly form was illuminated by a great light, and from her eyes beamed an intensity of pure love. With outstretched arms and looking beyond all surrounding objects, she kept her gaze on the one person present who was especially dear to her.

Watching her Molly was not frightened at all.

She was now witnessing with her eyes what she had always sensed to be true. Seamus's heart missed a beat when he heard Molly say:

'Mother, have you come for my baby?'

'No,' replied her mother tenderly, 'I've come for you.'

Instantly, Molly's spirit rose from her body and joining with her mothers they went towards the brilliant light and disappeared.

The wind continued to blow for a moment and then it was gone. When Seamus looked back at Molly body it was lying lifeless on the pillow.

'No Molly, no.' he cried as he rushed to her side. Trembling, he felt for her pulse but his impatient fingers could feel nothing. His stethoscope seemed stuck in his pocket as he tried to retrieve it.

yanking it free he placed it on her chest and strained his ears
at her heart beat. But there was only silence.

'No, Molly, not now, please God not now.'

Then he bent down to her lovely face. He heard a last deep intake
of breath and anxiously held his own. Slowly it came, Molly's last
sigh, deep and very slow. And as it left her mouth in that moment
Seamus knew she was gone.

Suddenly the sleeping baby moved beneath him and removing
Molly's heavy arm from around it he lifted it up.

The warmth of its little body drew large tears from his eyes.

He leaned over carefully and pressed it against Molly's lips as if to
let her kiss her child for the last time.

'Send for Fr. Brophy,' he said in a state of shock as he walked into
the kitchen moments later.

'Jesus, what is it?' David asked anxiously as he jumped up from the
chair, not even seeing the baby in his arms. Hattie moved closer to
Seamus and repeated the question:

'What is it son? What's wrong?'

Looking at them with tear filled eyes he said quietly: 'Molly is
dead.'

For a second, nobody moved, then Hattie reached over and took the
baby in her arms. David raced up the stairs two at a time, but on
reaching the bedroom, he stopped suddenly outside the door. He was
unable to go any further

Jessie followed quickly behind him. She was haunted by the
memory of what happened to
Molly's father all those years ago. Taking his hand she opened the
door and guided him towards the bed. Looking down at Molly's
lovely face, it was almost as if she was sleeping,

'David, you must say goodbye to her now,' said Jessie and with her
lips trembling she walked from the room. Once on the landing her
tears flowed as she broke down and wept.

Alone now with his darling Molly, David bent over and kissed her
lips, long and slow. They were still warm and became moist with his
tears. .

Taking her in his arms he said tenderly: 'Molly, my love, ah don't
go, don't leave me here all alone where I can't find you.'

Then looking up to Heaven he cried bitterly:

'I can't go on without you, I don't want to go on without you, darling you are my life,' and he stroked her lovely hair and kept stroking and kissing and talking to her in this way over and over, until his grief built up to an almost insufferable level.

When Jessie re-entered the room a little while later she found him rocking Molly to and fro as if to get some response from his beloved wife. Putting her hand on his shoulder she said quietly:

'Let her go David,' and she tried to pull him away.

'No Jessie, I will never let her go,' he said desperately and he turned and cried again into Molly's lifeless body. Pulling him back again Jessie took hold of his shoulders with both hands and spoke to him in a more serious way.

'Listen David,' she began,' you must listen to me now. Don't go and make a dreadful mistake all over again. That child downstairs has Molly's blood in it. She was born from the love you both had for each other. Put all your hope in her now. I know that is what Molly would have wanted.' David turned back and looked down at his love. Jessie watched him as he stroked her hair and kissed her for the last time. Then he took Molly's hands and tucked them under the bed- clothes, paused for a moment, slid his own hands into his trouser pockets and walked silently from the room.

Downstairs in the kitchen, Hattie sat nursing the sleeping baby in her arms. The same thoughts kept going round and round in her head.

What was it all about? What was it all for? Why Molly? She had everything to live for. She was young. Why not Hattie herself? Then she realised that she would never speak with her again. Oh, God she would miss her so much.

Tears ran down her cheeks. All she could see ahead of her was a deep black hole of despair. She began to tremble from weeping.

Suddenly the baby wriggled in her arms. Its little hand reached out and caught Hattie's finger, and in her grief Hattie held it tightly . It was then that she remembered the gypsy's prophecy

When David entered the kitchen Hattie struggled to stand up.

'No Aunt stay where you are,' he said concernedly as he placed his hand on her shoulder to prevent her from rising. Then he knelt down at her side. Wiping the tears from his eyes, he gently brushed the shawl away from the baby with the back of his fingers as if searching desperately for something. Then he saw it, Molly's very soul looking back at him through two little eyes.

CHAPTER FORTY THREE

William looked down from the pulpit and his eyes wandered slowly over the faces of Molly's family and friends. Fingering his papers he nervously began to speak;

'Dear friends,' he said in a low voice, 'if anyone had told me a week ago that I would be assisting Fr. Brophy at a funeral Mass for one of my dearest friends, I would not have believed it. And as I stand before you and look down at all the sad faces, I know exactly how you are feeling. Why?

Because I am feeling it too. I'm sad because I won't hear Molly's voice again or see her smile or watch her as she ran to me all excited about something. Yes, I will miss her, but for one reason only, and that is - Molly was alive.'

He paused for a few moments and when he continued his voice grew stronger, 'Molly did not half live or pretend to be. She lived her life, she loved her life. Of course she knew injustice and tried to help, she knew loneliness and sorrow too. But she did not make them her friends and go along their paths. For she was an exceptional girl.

She told me once, somebody said to her that she should be more hard of heart in order to survive a changing world.

But Molly replied that she preferred her own world for she had found love in it.

So dear friends, for Molly's sake, don't dwell on your mourning. Grieve for a time certainly, it is a necessary emotion, but then walk away and turn towards life. Don't let it drag you down into a grave of memories where you can only find joy in the past. Instead, pull yourselves up into the light.

Like Molly say 'yes' to love, and 'yes' to life.'

Then looking toward David he continued,

'There are people living who need us, and though we are in different bodies, yet in each one there is the same spirit. What we perceive to be dead in Molly, is as I speak, being born elsewhere. Life is a continuous force and to deny life is to deny love, and to deny love is to deny oneself, and to deny oneself is to deny God. So, today, as we say goodbye to our special friend Molly, we thank God for the time we had with her. Long or short it was a special time. She was

...que, she ... o ... utiful and she was ours.

There is ... ne thing left of the Molly we knew, that is her love and as yo... l well know my friends, real love never dies.'

David staied at the breast plate on the coffin and William's words awakened something in him stronger than faith. In that moment, the whole mystery of it all began unravelling in his mind. He remembered Molly's longing for her absent father. Her mother's presence in the wind.

Mick's warning on their wedding day. Jessie's insistence that she keep her name, her mysterious death and of course, their baby. Was this the love she spoke of? ... Of course, this must be the love she had left him.

The smoke from the holy incense encircled the coffin and drifted among the mourners awakening their senses. David, Seamus, Frank, J.J. and Walter stepped forward to carry Molly to her final resting place but they were a man short. Six men were needed. A frail old man stepped out of his seat and spoke to David.

'I would be honoured if you would let me help,' he said humbly.

'Thank you,' said David, 'puzzled as to his identity. It was Walkerton.

Each man stooped a little as they placed their shoulders under the hard wood, and supporting each other with their hands, they took their first step in unison and Molly's final journey began.

Wiping her tears away with a lace handkerchief,

Hattie followed, linked by Jessie and Doireann on either side.

A little behind them, a tall, well-built man escorted a woman who was obviously deeply distressed. She wore a tailored suit with an elegant hat perched on her short black hair. It was Roseanne.The procession paused at the back of the church and Molly's father stepped forward to relieve Walkerton. Walking out into the sunshine, David could hear Molly's words so clearly in his head:

'Oh David, no one will ever love you like I do.' and the tears that he had held back all morning filled his eyes and flowed down onto the ground.

In the graveyard the cortege stopped where a large hole had been dug out. The grave-diggers removed their hats and bowed their heads. The men lowered the coffin to the ground and stepped back. Jessie leaned forward and William watched as she placed Molly's ivory missal on the coffin. Standing alone, he began prayers in this way taken from the Latin ...

'Eternal rest grant unto her O Lord and may perpetual light shine upon her and . .'before he could finish, the breeze blew open the pages of the missal. Leaning forward to close it William noticed something pressed between them. It was a dried flower, a rose, the stem wrapped in brown paper. His rose, the one he had given her all those years ago 'and may she...' but he could not continue as his voice broke and he wept openly in front of his congregation.

Seamus, realising that his brother was in difficulties began to say the rosary and the stunned congregation joined in.

A little way off Mick McCoy leaned against one of the tall trees which had guarded the dead for centuries.

He had seen it all before. He had felt the pain too. Wasn't it his own Molly that lay cold in the grave that their daughter was being laid in today. No, Mick had no tears, nobody was going to make him cry. They would not get through the wall he had built around himself down through the years. Nobody could hurt him again, his heart was like stone.

When the prayers were over the grave-diggers lowered the coffin into the ground. David broke off a flower from his wreath and watched it as it floated down to land on Molly's name. The rest of the family did likewise.

The prayers were continued as the grave-diggers filled in the grave, and the thump of clay sounded so final as it landed on the coffin lid.

Soon a carpet of fresh flowers covered the grave at David's feet, a sign of how much Molly was loved. People shook his hand and went their way until he stood alone.

'I love you, Molly,' he whispered and turned and carried away her memory in his heart.

As he walked towards the gates, suddenly a hand reached out and grabbed his arm. David, being miles away in thought, jumped frightendly. When the strong stale smell of alcohol drifted into his nostrils he knew it had to be Mick McCoy.

'Ya should a listened ta me,' he said breathing heavily into David's face, 'I told ya what would happen, but no, you young people think ya know everything, you'll have to leave this place and do what I did wh͟ my ͟ ͟w͟ent. You'll have ta go to sea. Aye, the sea judges ͟ ͟no ͟efrien ͟ ͟o man, but it will carry ya from anything.'

Looking ...to Mick's dark empty eyes, David began to see the self-inflicted suffering and the hell he had lived in all those years. He tried to step away from Mick as he continued in a voice which had lost all hope,

'when you've sat night after night on the top deck of a ship surrounded by the cold hard pains of loneliness, then you will know the harm ya done. You may drown your sorrows and drink, and drink 'till ya can feel no more. Leave the child behind, for the curse of the Malone's is in the child.'

That was enough, when David heard the word 'child', an angry determination rose up in him.

'Why you pathetic stupid old man,' he said 'I could never be like you. I could not run and I will not hide, nor will I go to sea and lose myself in drink. Why, you thought only of yourself when you ran out, you didn't know what it was you had. The curse is not in the child you blind fool, the curse is in the father if he lets it. The love you lost in your wife was carried on in your child but you hadn't the guts to face it. It was easier to run and let someone else do that. All those years Molly wondered and longed to meet you and now it is too late. Well, it's not too late for me. I will go to my child and if I never give her anything, I will give her love. I will break this curse, as you call it, with love. I will cover it and smother it until it will be no more, and the love for my child shines as brightly as the sun.'

Then he went to walk away, but with the anger still raging inside him he stopped suddenly, turned, and grabbed Mick by the scruffy collar of his coat.

'And as for you,' he said with great contempt, 'You should be down on your knees at that grave begging her forgiveness. 'Then he let him go abruptly, 'but maybe it was better she never knew what her father was like after all,' and he walked away with his anger giving way to tears.

Mick McCoy stood shivering at the gate. He suddenly felt very cold. His withered hands trembled as he fumbled with the buttons on his jacket. He gave up and just held it tightly to his throat. For once in his miserable life, he did not know which way to turn.

Out on the street, Roseanne, a little stooped from grief, was just about to step into a waiting car. From the corner of her eye she saw Tom O' walking towards her.

'Roseanne, is that you?' he asked nervously, as he came closer. 'My God but you are a sight for sore eyes. How long are you home for? You know I tried to find you after but nobody knew where you were. Still, you're here now and it's great to see you.'

Then, placing his large hand on her thin arm his voice took on a more urgent tone.

'I really have to talk to you Rosy, when would we be able to get together?'

A wiry grin spread across Roseanne's tearstained face. In the intervening years since she had seen him, he seemed to have lost whatever had attracted her to him in the first place. Straightening her back she said quietly;

'So you want to get together Tom O', do ya?

Well you're seven years too late. You're too late for me and for the son you'll never see.'

Then, reaching into her black crocodile skin bag she pulled out an object with her gloved hand.

'See this do ya? Well ya dropped this the day you ran out on me in Bewleys. I found it and kept it all this time, just to remind me never to make the same mistake again with scum like you.' and she pushed the lighter into his hand.

'There, take it, and remember the next time you drop something precious, there'll always be someone smarter than you to pick it up.'

Then looking across the car at her escort she stepped into the car, banged the door and without another glance drove confidently away.

CHAPTER FORTY FOUR

David rooted anxiously through the drawers of the large oak chest. As he continued looking for something, he lifted out Molly's neatly folded clothes and held them close to his face. The scent of her perfume was still in the fabric, and as he buried his face in them he felt very close to her.

Then putting them back in the drawer, he closed it slowly, and decided that it would be better for him, if he gave them away. It seemed to him there would be something wrong, if he were to cling to her things, in order to remember her love. After all, Molly's heart was always full of freedom. Then, pulling out a smaller drawer, he was at last glad to have found what he was looking for.

As he held up the chain with the miraculous medal, he thought about his own mother, then Aggie, and how she gave it to Molly that day in Wexford. He smiled as he remembered the way Molly had admired it on the way home in the car.

God that all seemed such a long time ago now. He knew deep down that Molly would have wanted their daughter to have it, especially today at her christening.

An hour later he called in next door and collected J.J. and Jessie from the house. When they arrived over at no. 28, Hattie, Julie, Doireann and Seamus's new girlfriend Eithne were fussing over the baby, while Seamus and Walter sat calmly watching them as they enjoyed a smoke Jessie picked up the baby in her arms. She looked so beautiful in her christening robes

Taking the chain and medal from his pocket David reached over and fastened it around the baby's neck. Then he kissed her tenderly. There was an awkward silence, broken only by J.J. as everyone looked on.

'Ahem,' coughed J.J.

'What time do we have to be at the church?'

Twenty minutes later when they arrived in Meath street, Fr. William was waiting to greet them at the door of the church. Walking up the steps, Hattie was so proud to be the one chosen to carry Molly's baby. Carefully she handed her over to William at the old marble font. It was his first christening ceremony and Molly's baby made it extra special.

Back at number 28, Julie had a celebration buffet lunch ready for them when they returned.

On entering the house Hattie immediately put J.J. in charge of the drinks. Soon the house was full of family, friends and neighbours all celebrating. And after the sadness of the past few weeks, a great atmosphere of joy was welcomed by all. Then towards the end of the meal, Fr. William asked everyone to raise their glasses and join him in a toast to little Molly's health.

Afterwards Jessie sat waiting for a chance to talk to David alone. When it finally came she went over and sat beside him. Holding his daughter, he watched her as if, should he close his eyes she might disappear.

'I hope you don't mind David,' she said awkwardly 'but I know Molly would have wanted her to have these.'

She opened her hand and revealed Molly's wedding and engagement rings. Staring in disbelief he held out his hand and she placed them in his palm. Clutching them tightly, he closed his eyes and held them to his chest.

As he opened his eyes he released a tear and looking at her, he said gratefully;

'Thanks, I would never have thought of that.'

Later when everyone sat relaxed and chatting, the door of the sitting room opened slowly. Before anyone could say a word, Julie had shown Mick McCoy in. Hattie looked over at him in bewilderment.

Dressed in a dark suit and a starched white shirt, he fingered his hat nervously and said in a humble low voice: 'God bless all here .'

Hattie sat holding the baby tightly and she scowled at him as he awkwardly crossed the room and came towards her.

In a slight state of shock everyone watched David's reaction when they heard Mick say:

'It's alright ma'am, I'm the child's grandfather.'

Then, kneeling down on one knee he placed a silver coin in the baby's hand.

'That's for luck' he said as he touched the child's forehead.

Then trembling a little he looked around for a chair. Standing up, he walked over to the nearest one and sat down. Jessie came up behind him and squeezed his shoulder firmly.

'I'll be alright, sis,' he said quietly as he patted her hand.

o ... effort it must have taken to do what he did J.J. called to his ...ther in law,

' Nould ya like a drink Mick?'

Immediately the old sea dog's eyes lit up and clapping his rough hands together he replied gratefully,'

'I would J.J... I'd love a cup of tea.'

EPILOGUE

Six years later the heavy grey door of number 28 opened slowly and a little girl came bouncing down the steps.

Her long black hair hung loosely around her shoulders.

Hattie, dressed in a white silk blouse, designer slacks and a rather out of place apron, called after the child.

'Wait, don't forget your hat, Molly.'

Flicking her fringe back with her small hand, the child put her arms out, and as if she was embracing the whole world she said happily:

'No, Auntie, I like the wind to play in my hair.'